ORC'S MATE

A MONSTER MATE HUNT PREQUEL

AVA ROSS

ENCHANTED STAR PRESS

For my own special hero,
my husband, Rusty.

MONSTER MATE HUNT TERMS, CHARACTERS, & GENERAL IFORMATION

Orc's Mate (takes place 5 years before Orc's Craving):

Zephyr Clan: Air. Pendant is a circular disc made up of swirls to represent the air and water

Characters: Odik Brunellon, Eleri. Their children: Zur, Yusta

Birgid: woman who taunts Eleri and murdered Zur, the hunter who raised Eleri

Cassatine: orc midwife

Crikin: Dakur's father

Drabass: male from Odik's clan

Madine: elderly orc female; the keeper of clan stories

Trilden: Odik's friend

Zarran: Odik's vox

Zur: elderly man who adopted Eleri. They name their son after him

Orc's Craving, Book 1

Azuris Clan: Water/Sea. Pendant: metal swirls with spikes resembling waves

Characters: Rhoslyn, Jaus Kreedaull, Shirra: their daughter

Arkest: oldest, most revered healer

Eamon: village mayor who wants Rhoslyn for himself

Feyla: Jaus' female vox

Kael: older guardsman

King Surled: Jaus & Madr's father

Liall: older orc who runs an herb shop in the orc city

Lyneth: Rhoslyn's sister; married to Sveth

Mastivule: head of the kingdom's guards

Viskeete: rather crude orc

Orc's Fate, Book 2

Lumen Clan: sun/mountains. Pendant: shaped like the sun, it represents the mountains and the heavens above

Characters: Madr Thourand, Lyneth

Brakkis: Madr's vox

Finsteg: Matis Clan male who challenges Madr

Grock: Azuris clan male who guards Lyneth and is murdered

Kael: older village guardsman, friend to Lyneth

Milllamay: shayde Dakur raised

Pulost: Matis Clan male who challenges Madr

Riank: Madr's cousin who wishes to rule

Sessavia: Matis Clan female, welcomes Lyneth

Taen: shayde Dakur raised

Tenkaril: Madr's mother, adopted Zickar; wise woman who "sees" when she touches someone

Tescall: Riank's younger brother and ally

Orc's Maiden, Book 3

Matis Clan: forest. Pendant: spikes from the sun like sunlight stabbing through the canopy

Characters: Zickar, Alwen, their son: Ferrin

Bredar: Alwen's brother

Brillie: Flazant female

Creea: Alwen's sister

Dillu: Flazant male

Loobek: orc male who went looking for Dakur

Mavileen: human woman, leader of the village on the edge of the forest

Nayleen: Alwen's sister

Noul: one of three shaydes Dakur raised

Pirrah: Flazant elder

Roolina: Alwen's mother

Rusket: older orc male

Trillie: Flazant female

Ulong: orc metal worker

Villadeer: Flazant female

Wambak: Flazant male

Orc's Captive, Book 4

Matis Clan

Characters: Dakur, Nia

Brunt: Nia's stepbrother

Kengart: head of Brunt's guards

Lianire: Brunt's second in command

Veegar: human male, cook

Woobedon: Nia's village built in the middle of the vast desert, near an oasis

Orc's Taming, Book 5

Ember Clan: desert/fire. Pendant: flames shooting toward the sky

Characters: Turren, Kaila

Airest: Turren's vox

Brunnen: Kaila's younger brother

Daskin: Turren's second in command

Ferella: female orc, Ember Clan

Gromget: orc game that's a mix of soccer and American football

Jabon: Kaila's boss in the village

Nuark: teenage orc living in the Ember Clan

Reven: teenage orc living in the Matis Clan

Sianna: orcling infant

Urlain: elder in the Ember Clan

Varalar: female smithy at the village

Vox history: Winged creatures fostered in the Ember Clan and bonded with orcs. They form within a seed and when they slip out, they bond with the person closest to them. In earlier days, this was their parent, but now all eligible males and females travel to the Ember clan to be there for the hatching. The bonded orc remains with the hatchling long enough for the vox to grow for flight, feeding and grooming it so it knows their touch and smell. They nest near their bonded orc but return to the Ember territory every three years when they're ready to produce young.

General Terms:

Ashenclaw: creature like a wolf

Aspest berries: found on Odik's island, can be added to tea

Avestilar: large birds who nest high in the canopy

Boolong: creature like a wild cow

Brugel: meat like bacon

Caedos: leader of a clan

Chall: like a cat; kits are their young

Cheerish: type of bird

Clik: distance; about a mile

Daphoon: a dolphin-like sea creature

Doonet: a light cloth made from a plant

Dresalod: vicious, enormous crab-like sea creatures that attack the orc city

Elkern: timid creature like a deer

Effervast trees: fragrant

Emerest stone: rare, found in caverns, Turren compares the color to Kaira's eyes when she's angry

Fillawate: drink made from a rare fruit that grows deep beneath the ground. When fermented and drank, makes someone feel happy, though it's not alcohol

Flazant: stone people born of the boulders around us. Prior allies to the orcs

Hilardep: enormous, venomous spider found in the forest

Lamest: forest snake

Liladek flowers: lovely scent, bloom at night

Lindenmint: herb Rhoslyn drinks as tea; has antibacterial properties, slows a cut's blood flow. Found to be highly toxic to dresalods

Mellabar: a fruit jam

Orcling: orc baby/child

Reskit: creature like a rabbit

Ribber: creature like a rat

Secondist: Tuesday

Shayde: large, vicious, lizard-like creatures who live and hunt in the forest

Sinderfluff: material like silk

Squitt: creature like a squirrel

Succire, a sweet red berry

Tartledge Sea: vast, purple sea beyond the Orc Kingdom

Teegar: plants used to propel orcs to canopy platforms or take them below ground. Serve as elevators. Fed with diluted fillawate.

Teetser: a fly/mosquito

Trulist: trees that grow in thick groves

Wanderer: orc who travels, learning new ways to use their pendants

Weelen leaves: used in tea

Whisp: an insect that, when blown across, lights up. Used in lanterns as a source of light.

Willadon: a black root, made into a tea that relieves arthritis pain

Also by Ava Ross

Mail-Order Brides of Crakair

Brides of Driegon

Fated Mates of the Ferlaern Warriors

Fated Mates of the Xilan Warriors

Holiday with a Cu'zod Warrior

Galaxy Games

Alien Warrior Abandoned/

Shattered Galaxies

Beastly Alien Boss

Bride of the Fae

A Sci-Fi Holiday Tail

Monsterville, USA

Monster on Board

(co-written with Alana Khan)

A Monster Worth Fighting For

(Monster Between the Sheets)

Love at First Orc

Monster Mate Hunt

Brides of the Zuldrux Warriors

Single Titles

A Monster Worth Fighting For

Craving Stardust

Dad Bod Dragon

Mated to the Dragon

Jasmine's Enchanted Genie

Swamp Thing (You Make My Heart Sing)

You can find her books on Amazon.

ORC'S MATE

On the night of the Monster Hunt, an orc will claim me as his bride.

Eleri

When I'm falsely accused of murder, I steal the place of one of the women chosen for the Monster Mate Hunt. Each year, two of us must give ourselves to the orcs in exchange for their protection. I'm captured by Odik, the fierce leader of the Zephyr Clan.

He takes me to his island home far out to sea where he tells me he won't claim me until I've fallen in love with him. There's something powerfully attractive about this strong orc that I can't seem to resist. Soon, I'm not only falling for Odik, but I'm also savoring sharing my life with him.

Odik

When my clan pendant flared, it meant Eleri was my fated mate, the woman I'll love for a lifetime. She's skittish and shy, and I'll do anything to keep her safe. But with a storm approaching the island, threatening my clan and our very existence, we must work together to survive. After that, I'll show her how precious she is to me—then claim her as my bride.

Orc's Mate is set in the Monster Mate Hunt Series and takes place five years before Orc's Craving. Expect fated mates, found families, a distinctive size difference, and a "touch her and die" hero. Each book is standalone, but the series is best if read in order.

Books in Order:
Orc's Mate (Prequel)
Orc's Craving
Orc's Fate
Orc's Maiden
Orc's Captive
Orc's Taming

CHAPTER 1

ELERI

On the evening of the Monster Mate Hunt, I walked as fast as my bad leg allowed through the dimly lit streets of our village, a sack with my meager purchases banging against my thigh.

Tonight, two unfortunate women would be forced to leave the protection of our fortress walls. They'd run through the forest, hoping to hide, but it would be futile. Enormous, brutish orcs would hunt them, determined to claim them as a bride.

No one knew for sure what happened after they were caught by an orc, but the whispered, horrifying stories were enough to make women get down on bended knees to beg the fates not to be chosen.

Exhaustion threatened to drag me down onto the cobblestone street, but I'd long since learned not to show I was in pain. Weakness was either exploited or scorned here.

My leg wasn't the only part of me that hurt, though that was a constant ache I did my best to ignore. My eyes burned from focusing on tiny stitches, and my fingertips stung from wielding the sewing needle to the point it shredded my skin.

In the forest beyond the high stone walls, a shayde shrieked. I froze much like I must've done when my parents abandoned me in the nearby forest when I was three; after it was clear my leg no longer worked as it should. It had been twenty-two years since that day, and I could no longer remember how I was injured. And since my parents lived in a distant village, I couldn't ask.

If Zur hadn't been hunting that night and heard my whimper of fear, the shaydes would've consumed me like they had so many of my fellow villagers who'd strayed beyond the stone fortress walls after dark.

"Hurry up there, Eleri," Birgid called out from the open doorway of one of the wooden houses lining both sides of the street, and I scooted forward. "If you keep going at your current pace, it'll take you all night to get home." The cruel laughter of her friends punctuated her words. Until they'd decided it would be fun to mock me, they'd probably been gossiping about the hunt. They should be fretting about which young women would be chosen—maybe even one of them—rather than bothering with me.

From the moment I'd arrived here, three years old to their five, they'd hounded me, begging the mayor to send me back to the forest where the shaydes would finish me off.

"What a useless thing you are," one of the other women said. "Look. She can barely move."

Birgid hooted. Her gaze shot down the alley where my friend, Zur, waited in our tiny home. "We should shove her out the front gates tonight to placate the orcs instead of giving them one of our own."

I am one of their own, I thought fiercely, though I bit down on my tongue to keep from speaking.

An enormous forest that went on for so many cliks surrounded my village, and no one had ever spanned the entire distance. Over a thousand human villagers hid beyond each ring of high fortress walls, relying on fierce, enormous orcs who granted us protection from the shaydes, creatures even more dangerous than themselves.

The orcs didn't do this out of the goodness of their hearts.

In exchange, they demanded *brides.*

As I left the evil women behind, their cackles stabbed through the humid air. I scurried past the alley containing my home and continued three blocks to the butcher's shop, hoping to find a bargain on a small piece of meat. I wanted to make a hearty stew with the vegetables in my bag. Zur would enjoy it, and his warm smile would make everything all right again like it had every day since he adopted me as his own.

Once I'd made a purchase, a measly bit of fatty meat, unfortunately, I returned to the alley and hurried to the rickety home I shared with Zur.

More laughter rang out from Birgid's friends. I wasn't

sure where Birgid was, but I'd keep a sharp watch in case she crept up behind me.

Pitiful thing, one of them said.

Useless for anything but sewing, another added.

And *Toss her out the gate.*

It was all I could do to keep my spine straight and my chin held high. I might not walk well, but no one would disagree that I was the best seamstress in town. Even my boss would say so, though she'd yet to pay me with enough coin to buy me and Zur more than a few skimpy meals. He hunted and I worked each day of the week, but it was all we could do to make the rent on the small hut where he'd so kindly raised me.

He was the only person I would ever trust.

The sun slid closer to the horizon, casting long shadows that whispered secrets among the cobblestones. Today had been especially grueling at the seamstress's shop, where I'd worked tirelessly on delicate embroidery that would be taken for granted by those who donned the garment. I doubted they took even one moment to appreciate whose nimble fingers had crafted each stitch.

At least I had coins to buy our meal. I needed to remember that and not think of how badly my back ached.

As I approached the simple home where Zur and I lived, I picked up my pace to a moderate hobble. He was more than just a guardian; he'd become my father and my solace amidst the scornful gazes and whispers plaguing my every step. His warmth and wisdom provided a sanctuary within those walls, shielding me from the cruel world outside. I couldn't wait to see his cheerful smile and share the news of our day.

Scraping sounds rang out behind me near the head of the alley. My skin flashed with goosebumps, and I spun, but I didn't see anyone there. Even better, no rock sailed my way, ready to hit me and leave a bruise.

The light had faded, however, and with carts parked along the side and refuse strewn in between, almost anyone could be hiding.

"Hello?" I called out.

Only silence greeted me—and the feeling of being watched.

"Get inside," I hissed. "Ignore whatever it might be."

With a shake of my head, I pushed open our front door and stepped inside.

"I talked the butcher into lowering his price for a good piece of meat," I called out happily as I closed the door behind me. "I'll make soup, and the vegetables I bought on my way home will round out our wonderful dinner." There was nothing I enjoyed more than cooking Zur a satisfying meal. At eighty, he deserved good food, lots of rest, and plenty of time to chat with his friends. Instead, he spent too much time hunting in the forest to provide for a woman who maybe *should've* been left behind to die.

I hurried through the darkened interior toward the tiny kitchen to prepare our meal but stumbled over something big and solid lying across the floor. Falling to my knees beyond it, I gasped as pain shot through my limbs.

The sack containing our meal had split open from the impact, exposing the meat. Blood leaked around it—

I blinked slowly, trying to process what I was seeing.

The circle was too large to have come from our meat.

Gulping, I scrambled away from the horrifying pool, falling onto my side when my right leg couldn't support my weight.

I swallowed hard while my pulse pounded in my ears. It was all I could do to turn toward the large object I'd tripped over.

Only dim light filtered through the waxed paper window, but it was enough to see.

My gasp echoed in the quiet room.

Zur lay lifeless on the floor, his wide, shock-filled eyes glazing over already. Blood seeped from where someone had sliced through his throat enough to expose his windpipe. A wicked knife lay on the floor beside him, glinting in the flickering light of the whisp lantern he must've lit to provide a beacon to guide me home.

The whisp needed someone to blow on it or it would soon go out—such an inane thought to have when my world was falling apart.

My guttural cry of dismay rang out.

"Zur. Please, no." Tears stabbed the back of my eyes, and I cried out again, my voice hoarse and guttural.

Through the murky window, a flash of movement caught my eye. Whoever it was slithered into the gathering darkness on the side of the alley.

A cackle I'd recognize anywhere echoed in the stillness.

Birgid.

She'd hated me since we were schoolgirls and for such silly reasons.

The teacher called on me instead of her.

I found a coin on the cobblestone street where she'd just passed.

A cute boy winked my way when she wanted him. She's won him, married him, bedded him even, but that wasn't enough. She wanted me stomped to the ground. Completely defeated. Thrown out of the village.

I could see where this would soon lead. Panic surged up my throat along with rank bile. I grabbed the cold metal knife and rose to my feet, rushing to the window. I strained to catch a glimpse of her returning, but the alley was clear.

I sobbed as I hurried back to Zur.

"Zur, please wake up." I dropped to my knees beside him, unable to breathe. But he was too long gone to hear me. My wretched cries filled the room as I mourned his loss.

This man had loved me when no one else did. How would I go on without him?

The door opened behind me, and someone rushed inside. "What's going on? Zur? Has that woman—"

One of Birgid's friends groaned and started vomiting, splattering it everywhere. Other villagers crowded into our tidy home, gathering around me and Zur much like the blood that continued to seep into the floorboards I'd washed myself last night.

Birgid slunk in last, her face wreathed with innocence.

"She killed him," she bellowed, and the accusation was echoed by the others.

Murderer.

Fiend.

She must be punished for what she's done to that poor, poor soul who only showed her kindness.

Fear constricted my throat, denying me the wind to utter even one word in my defense. I doubted they'd listen even if I could find the will to speak. They'd convicted me already, and soon, they'd make sure I paid the final price.

While Birgid released a subtle smile, the others stomped toward me, each face twisted with anger, their hands lifted to form claws. The walls I'd trusted to protect me were crumbling, exposing the darkness lurking inside those Zur and I had called our friends and neighbors.

I rose to my shaky feet and the knife slipped from my grip, clattering on the wooden floorboards.

Spinning, I hobbled out the door and moved as quickly as I could down the street.

The open front gate loomed not far ahead. Two women stood just inside, their families clinging to them, pleading for someone to intervene.

They'd been chosen for the Monster Mate Hunt.

While villagers screamed for my capture behind me, I somehow found the strength to outdistance them.

I rushed toward the young women, grabbing a bag from one of them as I passed. With my lungs on fire, I rushed to the open fortress door.

"I'll take the place of one of you," I called out as I slipped through the opening and hurried across the big open field between the fortress walls and the looming forest.

The voices grew in volume behind me but for the first time, they couldn't do a thing to cause me harm. They might wish to capture and punish me, but no one would dare leave the village now that the sun had set.

"Run, murderess," Birgid called out from the top of the wall. "Run fast and far, and never come back or we'll make you pay."

I sent her a glare, but it felt weak and useless —like me.

With my pulse thundering in my ears, I slipped among the trees.

If the shaydes didn't get me, I'd soon be claimed as an orc's bride.

CHAPTER 2

ODIK

I crouched high in the trees on a thick branch, waiting for the fortress gate to open and gift two fortunate orcs with mates. Around me, other males from my Zephyr Clan and four to five males from each of the other five clans also waited.

Clutching my pendant, I sent the fates a wish. *Let her be one of them.*

The others talked, keeping their voices low, but they must've been asking the fates for the same thing.

"For five years, I've come to the hunt hoping to find a mate," one whispered. "For five years, my clan's pendant has not gifted me with the one I will adore until my dying day."

Drabass, a male from my clan, sighed. "It's the shaydes' fault. If they hadn't killed most of our precious females, we wouldn't need to come here and essentially beg the humans to reluctantly give women to us." A snarl ripped up his throat. "We should kill every shayde until none still survive."

"Then we'd never be gifted by a mate," another clansmale and my good friend, Trilden, said from beside me.

"I lost a mother. A sister. A wife," someone else said sadly. "Killing all the shaydes won't replace them."

"Nothing will replace those we lost," I said. There wasn't one orc who hadn't suffered after the shaydes attacked our clans at the same time five years ago.

"If the shaydes are no longer a threat, the humans won't beg for our protection." Trilden said. "They'll dissolve our treaty. They'll stop sending out two females each year for us to hunt as mates. In fact—"

Hearing a subtle sound, I held up my hand, and everyone froze.

Three shaydes slunk across the forest floor, crossing right below us, their glowing red eyes flicking around. They sought prey, but they would go hungry tonight.

Despite being almost as large as an orc, their clawed footsteps were nearly silent on the leaf-strewn path.

We watched, not speaking or even moving as they passed, their thick scaled tails sweeping back and forth as they slunk deeper into the woods.

Once they were gone, we relaxed—somewhat—and waited for the fortress gate to open and for two lovely females to emerge.

"Do you think you'll hunt tonight?" Trilden whispered. "You're caedos, leader of the Zephyr Clan. Surely the fates will grant you a bride. You need an orcling to take your place when you get old."

"I hope so." Prayed so.

"*I* will happily hunt," Drabass said with a tusk-filled grin, grabbing his crotch.

I growled, and his shoulders slumped. He dropped down to sit on the branch, watching the gate.

Trilden huffed and kept his voice low so only I could hear. "He bears watching."

"All the time." Drabass's father had sought to lead our clan when my father died. We'd fought, and I'd won. He'd accepted the outcome of the match, and he'd been a good friend since, but Drabass had never accepted that he would not be in line for the role.

Truly, it was more a burden than a gift, as he'd see if he did more than behave in a jealous manner.

Trilden's gaze took in my pendant much like his own, a circular disc made up of swirls. Zephyr meant air, and long ago, my people chose the symbol and the clan name to represent how we lived at the top of the cliffs of a small island far out to sea. The shaydes, thus far, hadn't swum out to the island, and we built our homes high enough, it was rare we suffered from a dresalod attack. The sea creatures more frequently attacked the city and sometimes even those living in the hills beyond.

Ocean beasts with vicious claws and an appetite for our flesh, dresalods could scale almost any surface. We'd long since perfected our skill with a bow and arrow, shooting them off the cliffs before they reached us.

Because of that, they hadn't breached the cliffs in almost a year.

Trilden slapped my back. "I wish you luck, friend." He truly meant it.

"The same to you," I said.

"They come," another called out in a low voice.

We turned as one to watch. Anticipation skipped through my veins. Would I be chosen this time, or would I have to return a year from now and lift my hopes once more?

Only one woman rushed through the opening in the gate. She moved quickly across the field and into the woods.

"She has an irregular pace," Trilden said, though not with scorn. When you lose so many of your people, you treasure those who remain no matter what their abilities.

"A limp won't keep her from bearing orclings," Drabass said with a low, barely audible laugh.

My sharp look made him snap his mouth shut, but nothing would silence this male. One day, I feared this festering wound between us would crack open and pus would seep out. Then I'd have to take care of it permanently.

We stopped breathing as the woman passed beneath us, each of us scanning the others for the sign that would tell us who would be chosen to pursue her.

That's when my Zephyr pendant flared, the swirled tips blazing brightest.

The others huffed and shook their heads. They

dismissed the first female and turned hungry gazes to the gate where the second would appear.

Trilden shot me a grin. "Go collect your mate. She belongs solely to you."

With my heart soaring all the way to the sky, I leaped off the branch, landing lightly on the ground.

Then I took off after the female, eager to claim her.

CHAPTER 3
ELERI

Fear coursed through my veins as I hobbled through the dense forest, trying to find a path with only the light of the sketchy moonlight filtering through the trees above. My right leg protested each step. I'd long since accepted my leg would never perform the way I wanted, but it burned in my belly that even in this, the time when I needed it most, it still failed me.

With each blink of my eyes, I saw Zur lying dead on the floor again, and it was all I could do to keep from sobbing. But something like that would draw attention.

If I let my sadness consume me, I'd collapse. Then the orcs would find me—or something equally horrifying.

Twigs and leaves crunched beneath my feet, and the sound of my erratic heartbeat was a steady thrum in my ears. I slowed my pace. Better to move carefully than announce to the world I was here.

"You think the orcs didn't see you leaving the

fortress?" I whispered as I stumbled over a branch I didn't see in time. With a wrench to the left, I caught myself before falling to my knees. Each of my gasping breaths felt strained, as if the air was thick with dread, adding weight to my chest.

A low, rumbling growl reverberated through the trees, making my blood run cold. Pausing, I peered around, searching for the source but seeing nothing but shadows flickering, mocking my vulnerability. Shivers rippled across my skin, but I kept going. If I could find a place to hide, I could stay there until morning. The shaydes would return to their dens, and the orcs would leave the area, right?

I didn't know the answer to that question.

I couldn't return to the fortress. My way out of the trap I'd found myself in was through the woods. Would another village take me in if I told them what happened?

If my friends and neighbors believed I was a murderer, so would strangers.

I reached a small clearing peppered with new growth trees and started weaving through them to reach the other side.

Rustling echoed in the bushes along the edge, and I froze, a deer locked in place by terror.

A pack of hungry ashenclaws emerged from the thick woods; surrounding me before I could make a peep.

My heart leaped into my throat, choking off my wind, and I backed against a sturdy tree. I looked up quickly to see if I could reach a branch and pull myself out of their reach, but the branches were too high to reach.

The ashenclaws' eyes gleamed with merciless hunger and were fixed on me like a pack of relentless demons thirsting for fresh prey. Panic clawed at my chest, urging me to flee, but my leg would continue to betray me. There was no way I could outrun them.

Spying a stick lying on the ground, I hefted it and swung it in a circle, brandishing it like I could actually use it to defend myself.

They stalked closer, encircling me in a noose. The tops of their heads came to my mid-chest, and their thick, ashen gray fur that gave them their name glistened in the moonlight. Claws as long as my pinky finger dug into the soil as their muscles bunched in preparation to lunge toward me.

Predators, they hunted in packs, their vicious teeth hamstringing prey. When the victim fell, they'd rip out their throat.

Then, they'd feast. It didn't matter if the person was still alive.

I tried to swallow, but the mass of fear in my throat kept it from going down.

The hoots and shouts of orcs hunting a bride echo through the trees, mingling with the ashenclaws' low growls. Fate itself was conspiring against me, forcing me into a situation with no way out. Tears blurred my vision, but I sniffed them away. If I went down, it would only be with a fight.

The ashenclaws tightened their circle, snapping their

jaws with hunger. I poked the stick toward the one closest in a futile attempt to intimidate it. But the rest only grew bolder, their feral eyes narrowing on me. Their heavy paws brought them so close, the rank smell of their breath clouded my senses.

I'd fight them off as long as I could. Even when my parents abandoned me, I hadn't given up. Only now did I remember grabbing a stick then like I did today, determined to do all I could to survive.

A fierce growl pierced through the darkness on my right, and an orc stalked from the forest into the open area.

He leaped up and over the line of ashenclaws like a vengeful deity, a thick staff in his hand.

His eyes locked on me with an intensity that sent both fear and relief coursing through my veins. I'd either have my throat ripped out by the ashenclaws or I'd be claimed by this orc—this I knew in my heart.

Gnashing his tusks, the orc charged at the menacing ashenclaw pack, swinging his weapon with lethal precision. The crack of the staff against snarling jaws echoed through the stillness, shattering the grip of terror holding me captive. In this violent dance between predator and predator, he was my unexpected savior—a fierce warrior protecting what he must see as his future bride.

My breath caught as I watched him leap and strike, each powerful blow unleashing a wave of wild, desperate energy that ignited my instincts. His long black hair tinted with unexpected green swung across his shoulders, and his thick muscles bulged beneath his greenish-gold skin as he relentlessly defended me.

This is not the orc my village told stories of—an untamable monster—but a guardian driven by something I couldn't define. I was torn between running from the ashenclaws and my unexpected need to protect the enormous male risking his life to save mine.

His smooth skin glistened in the moonlight. He released a battle cry and vaulted at one ashenclaw after another, showing a breathtaking display of strength and agility.

When only one ashenclaw remained standing, the orc stalked toward it.

"Dare me, beast," he growled. "And face my wrath."

The creature leaped at the same time as the orc, and they crashed together. The orc's staff fell to the forest floor, and dressed only in a leather loincloth, he grappled with the ashenclaw. The beast's claws raked the orc's chest, but he didn't cry out. His thick arms bulged, and lines tightened on his face as he encircled the ashenclaw's throat.

Its teeth raked down the orc's face, but he never released his grip. He held on while the beast pummeled the orc's head, not releasing the creature until the light faded from its eyes and its body slumped.

The orc tossed the beast aside and whirled to face me, his thick green blood flowing freely from the wounds on his face, neck, and chest.

He stepped toward me, his hand stretched out like a plea, but toppled to the ground before he reached me.

I woke with a dull ache in my right temple, lying on the ground with my head resting on something soft. The full moon shone down on us, and the scent of earth and night-blooming blossoms filled the air. Opening my eyes, I found myself staring up into the woman's worried face. Her fingers gently traced across my brow, soothing my throbbing headache. A glance down told me she'd tended my wounds, somehow wrapping my chest with strips of fabric from the hem of her dress.

She was so tiny compared to me; I doubted the top of her head would reach my mid-chest. It must've been a challenge to shift me around to bandage my wounds.

"Are you alright?" she asked in the universal language. A hint of fear flitted through her rich brown eyes. Did she think I'd harm her?

Possibly. They treated us with respect tainted with

derision, and I'd heard they built huge, false stories about us and the hunt.

To think she hadn't fled after I defeated the ashenclaws. I admired her for remaining here to tend to me. And from my staff clutched in her hand, she'd also stayed here to *defend* me.

It was humbling to think this little human would do such a thing for me.

"I'm fine." My voice was gruff from the encounter with the ashenclaws and the awe I felt for my clan-chosen mate. "Thank you."

She tucked a strand of fiery red hair behind her ear, her eyes flickering with fear and determination.

"You're welcome. I'm Eleri," she whispered, barely audible.

"Odik."

She repeated my name and the sound of it on her lips made my body surge to life. I couldn't help but be drawn to her. I was captivated by her petite frame, her lush curves, and her courage.

My head pounded where the ashenclaw had hit me, but I couldn't continue lying on the warmth of her lap. Reluctantly, I rose to my feet and took my staff from her tight grip.

"I claim you in the name of the Zephyr Clan." I said solemnly. "You're mine, and nothing will ever part us."

A shiver tracked through her, but again, she didn't run. She rose to her feet and pressed her back against a tree.

The human women orcs claimed in prior hunts said they were told we'd drag them to the ground and immediately rut with them. Claim them in the most brutal way possible. That we were basically animals.

Had the villagers finally told the women that instead, we cherished them, treasured them? We loved them, and they soon felt the same, willingly bearing our orclings. Happily remaining by our sides.

I held my hand out to her. "Will you come with me to my home built on an island far out to sea?" I didn't share that as the clan caedos's mate, she'd be honored and respected. Better she sees this for herself. Then she'd believe.

She swallowed hard and pinched her hand against her side. "I don't . . . "Her gaze darted toward the direction she'd come from, and the fear grew in her eyes.

I reeled around but found nothing there.

"We need to leave this place before shaydes are drawn to the carcasses," I said. "They hunt at night, and the smell of blood fills the air."

"Where will you take me?" A quaver came through in her voice, and the sound wrenched through me. It was common for fated mates such as us to fall for each other quickly. Already, I felt drawn to her like no other.

"To Zephyr Clan territory. I promise you," I pressed my fist against my chest. "I will not harm you or touch you with anything but respect. Plus, I will only take things farther when you know me better." My heart beat faster than it should because I already *craved* her.

She placed her hand in mine, and my soul wrenched sideways. I felt as if the ground shifted beneath us, like the stars in the heavens split wide open and rained light down upon us.

As if my destiny was held in Eleri's tiny hand.

CHAPTER 5
ELERI

Why wasn't I running from him, shrieking in terror?

To be honest, when he fell at my feet, I contemplated fleeing. But he'd protected me from sure death, and how could I leave him when he was completely vulnerable?

Instead, I tore off the bottom of my skirt and bound his wounds, blotting the long, jagged mark on his face that would leave a scar, plus the gouges on his chest. Instead of making him appear even more feral, the mark on his face gave him a ferocious, hero-like appearance.

For whatever reason, the fates had decided he was my hero.

Assuming I could trust him. I'd go with him for now and decide later. It wasn't like I had options in the middle of the forest. I couldn't defend myself, but he'd already proven he would battle to protect me.

As I'd eased him up onto my lap and clutched his

staff, prepared to defend him if I could, a giddy laugh nearly burst from my throat. I bit it back, worried if I released it, I'd never stop cackling. I'd gone from finding my father dead to being accused of murdering him to sitting on the forest floor with an enormous orc's head in my lap as if we were out on a picnic and he'd fallen asleep.

His even breathing soothed me, and I focused on him rather than the bodies lying around us, but I was never more grateful when he woke and took his staff. I was no warrior. If anything, I was the weakest person in the village.

That's how I knew no male would ever want me.

When he announced I was his, something deep inside me blossomed. That part of me wasn't afraid. If anything, I was excited at the idea of belonging to someone who actually wanted me.

He wants a mate, I reminded myself. Not exactly me.

But when he vowed not to touch me until I was ready, I wanted to leap into his arms. Cling.

I had to be out of my mind. This was a brutish orc, the beast of my childhood nightmares. He was no savior, and he would grow impatient when I didn't give in. He'd claim me soon whether I told him I wanted it or not.

But I swear I saw kindness in his gorgeous golden eyes.

He led me through the forest, taking a path I only saw when he placed his feet on it. He kept peering around intently, but I didn't hear shaydes or more ashen-claws—yet.

We walked longer than I liked, his sharp gaze taking in everything around us, including the way I had to jerk my leg forward to keep up with his rapid pace.

"Are you injured?" he asked quietly.

"No, this is just . . . me."

"I see." His words came out clipped as if he was angry. I hoped not at me, though he probably was. Everyone grew impatient with me before too long. Except Zur. He was the only one who would slow his pace so I could keep up.

And now he was dead.

It was my fault. She'd killed him to get even with me.

"I was injured when I was little," I said. "I don't remember how it happened because I was only three at the time. It was horrible, though. The memory of the pain still wakes me up at night." The words tumbled out of me, a cringeworthy vomit because I was eager to get this over with. "I've got a scar on my thigh. It's big and pale and rippled. Whoever sewed my flesh together would never be capable of doing fine embroidery. I should know. I cast a fine stitch myself." My sigh ripped out of me. "Anyway. I haven't walked right since it happened."

"You walk like you. *Eleri*," he said gruffly. "That's good enough for me."

For now, at least.

As for the future? I knew how this would work out.

My heart pinched tight. Was it wise of me to see even a speck of good in this orc? Whenever I'd trusted someone in the past, they eventually mocked or scorned me.

Odik had claimed me as his mate, and it wouldn't be long until he drove his cock inside me. Would he care that I'd never been with a male, or would he rip through my maidenhead in his need to plant his orcling seed deep within me?

He looked down at our linked hands before his sharp eyes landed on my face. Terror had to be reflected there. It was so entrenched inside me; it made my body shake.

"I'm sorry I'm slowing us down," I said, my teeth chattering. "We're going . . . somewhere, and I assume my pace is keeping us from getting there in a timely manner."

"Never fear, little one." He swept me up in his arms, and his strides ate up the cliks. Would he carry me all through the night? It seemed so, because he kept going, his steps even and his lungs unlabored.

His warmth enfolded me. Surely it was wrong of me to snuggle into his chest and let myself doze.

I'd worked hard for twelve hours making fine stitching.

I'd gotten up at dawn to make Zur's breakfast—

Zur! my heart cried. I kept picturing him lying dead in his own blood. The sneer on Birgid's face. Me being accused of murdering him when Birgid was the one who'd wielded the blade.

I fell asleep, and nightmares took over. Only someone's soft murmurs soothed me.

I woke when Odik leaped up onto something and

settled me in his lap, his arms remaining protectively around me.

Looking down at what I now rode on, my eyes widened.

The enormous, green scaled beast we sat on leaped toward the sky, its long wings snapping out to catch the wind.

CHAPTER 6
ODIK

"I'm flying," Eleri cried out. "I'm flying!" Her arms lifted, and she tipped her head back against my chest. "I can't believe it. I haven't run since I was three but now I. Am. Flying!"

"You're not afraid," I shouted over the wind buffeting around us.

"Should I be?" She peered over her shoulder at me, and I swore I read mischief in her eyes. "You jumped up onto this thing and—"

"Vox."

"I'm sorry?"

"We're riding on a vox."

"And a lovely vox it is. Green scales. Who would've thought?"

"His name's Zarran." I wasn't sure what to make of my mate. She'd initially come along with me willingly, something I'd heard wasn't common. The other human females fought their mates at first. It took time and patience to show them they didn't need to be afraid.

Then she shared a bit of her past and fear seemed to consume her. She slept in my arms in a trusting way, but her sharp cries told me she had nightmares.

What kind of life had she led?

Now my mate was acting like she was on an adventure.

"Can I pet your vox later?" she asked.

"You're not afraid he'll bite your head off?"

Laughter bubbled in her voice. "Will he?"

"Of course not."

"Then why ask if I'm afraid of him hurting me? Obviously he won't or we wouldn't be riding him. You know him well enough to give him a name."

"I, yes, I do. I bonded with him from the moment he slipped from the seed. I worked hard with him, teaching him foot commands. He's a loyal, friendly vox."

She leaned back against me. "See? I knew I had nothing to be fearful of."

"You enjoy flying?"

"Well, I've never done it before. But it always takes me twice as long as everyone else to go from one location to another. My leg has held me back almost all my life. I love that I'm traveling through the sky on a great winged creature named Zarran and that I'm going somewhere quickly. It's quite freeing." She sucked in a deep breath and released it.

"I feel the same." A frown brewed on my brow. "Why aren't you afraid of *me*?"

"I'm sure I should be."

"Actually, you shouldn't. I told you I won't claim you as my mate until you're ready."

"And that's why I'm not afraid. Back in the village, everyone tells horror stories about orcs, how they're fierce beings—"

"We are."

"I could see that when you fought the ashenclaws. Watching you battle them was both exhilarating and astonishing."

"Why astonishing?"

"Everyone else would have run in the opposite direction."

"You're my mate. My fated one. My clan pendant chose you for me. I'd be a poor mate if I ran and didn't remain to defend you."

"What do you mean your clan pendant chose me for you?" She lifted her arms, tipped her head back with her eyes closed, and grinned.

I'd felt the same the first year or so I'd ridden Zarran —once I'd learned how to hold on and not fall off. When had I lost the joy of flight?

Perhaps when I took over the burden of leading my people.

Worry about that would consume me soon enough. For now, I nudged it aside to focus on my mate.

"Our pendants always choose." Realizing that wasn't much of an explanation, I continued, hoping I didn't bore her. "There are six orc clans, and each member wears a pendant with a different symbol. When we meet our fated one, our pendants flare. Mine did when you left the fortress."

"Ah, interesting. Magical?"

I shrugged. "No one knows why."

"I noticed your pendant has swirls."

"To represent air. I'm Caedos of the Zephyr Clan."

"Caedos?"

"Leader."

"Ah."

"What does ah mean?" Females were complicated creatures. Since the shaydes killed most of them five years ago, I'd only interacted with a few of them.

"It just means I assumed so. You have a commanding presence."

My chest puffed with pride. "Thank you."

"And you take charge quite easily."

She hadn't even seen me among my people, and she'd noted this already? My chest expanded further.

"As I said, Zephyr represents air," I said. "My people live on an island far out to sea that juts into the air."

"And your vox flies you from the shore to your home."

"We use voxes for transportation but also in battle."

"The shaydes are horrifying creatures."

"They killed most of our females. They've attacked us for many generations, but five years ago, they gathered into large packs and challenged us all at once. We lost many warriors but the worst thing of all was that they found the building where we'd hidden our precious females. They killed almost all of them."

"That's why you formed the treaty with us," she said, her fingers twitching where she'd laid them on her thighs.

"Your village needs protection, and we need orclings if our species is going to survive."

"Two women a year won't give you many orclings."

"It will have to be enough. We don't want to ask for more."

"Why not? I imagine the village would give you more if you demanded this from them."

"Because your population could not sustain more than two."

"That surprises me," she said. "There are over a thousand people in the village, and more women than men in general. I imagine we could give five or ten a year."

My mate was an interesting woman.

"We signed the treaty already. It would be wrong to ask for changes."

She shrugged. "Maybe come to the fortress walls and ask to speak to the women."

"Would they talk to us?" I couldn't imagine such a thing. They feared us. Cried out in terror when they saw us.

"If they knew you weren't horrifying beasts," she said. "Women might join you willingly."

"Would they?" I asked, skeptically. "We're big, green, and we have horns. We're not tiny and delicate like human females."

"We may appear delicate, but I bet we'd surprise you.

Most of us are tough on the inside, where it truly matters."

"I'm beginning to suspect you're right." With her, at least. Other orcs had not shared my experience with their mates initially. This made my heart lighten. Perhaps I'd find peace and comfort with my mate, not a battle like many others. I cleared my throat. "Why didn't you run when I collapsed?" Something that gravely embarrassed me, though I was not going to remind her. I'd never lost consciousness after a battle, and I hoped I never did again.

"Because you were injured. You didn't collapse. I suspect you were knocked out. Don't you remember the last ashenclaw battering your head?"

Vaguely. "I'd killed all the ashenclaws. If you'd fled, I'm sure I would've survived."

"If my guardian had left me in the forest when I was three, would I have survived?"

"You were young. Gravely injured."

"You were also gravely injured."

"You have a soft spot for those who need aid?"

She shrugged. "It didn't feel right to leave you."

Was the bond influencing her already? Those chosen by clan pendants fell for their mates quickly, and this had universally happened with the females sent from the fortress to be claimed.

I couldn't imagine anyone loving me other than through a sense of duty, like those I took care of back in my village. Something deep inside me ached to feel the love of someone special, however, a person who'd care for me when no one else could.

Was that Eleri? May the fates make it so.

"Tell me about the other clans. What symbols do they wear?" she asked.

"Those of the Basselt or earth Clan live within the heart of the enormous mountain range near our biggest city."

"In caves?"

"So I've heard. They say things glow there, but I can't imagine such a thing. I haven't visited. I prefer the sunshine and the sea." Even if the lack of rain was decimating my clan numbers. "Then we have the Azuris or water clan. They primarily live in the city built along the shore. My friend, Jaus, is the newly appointed commander of the military. When the dresalods attack, he leads the charge."

"I'm surprised your clan isn't Azuris since you live far out to sea."

"Clans were chosen many generations ago. Zephyr fits us."

"Ah."

Again, that ah, as if she was processing everything I said, though not judging. A feeling of contentedness settled over me, the first time I'd savored the feeling in ages. The weight of my people's survival had fallen on me when I was much too young to take on the mantle. My father died during the great shayde battle five years ago when I was seventeen, and only Crickin, Drabass's father, challenged me. My father had trained me well, and I won the match.

No one else had tried to claim leadership. Our life was tough, and eking out an existence on the islands was challenging enough without dealing with the day-to-day tasks of the caedos. Most could see that.

Not Drabass, but he was a fool. He'd make a horrible caedos, and despite not always wishing to have this role, the fates were wise when they chose me.

Now they'd proven their wisdom again with Eleri.

"The other clans include Lumen, for the sun," I said. "They live high in the mountains, and many are part of the royal family. The other two clans are the Malis or shadow clan who live in the forest, and the Ember or fire clan. They live beyond the mountains in a stark, dry climate. They foster our voxes."

"You travel there to claim one after it's hatched?"

"They form within a seed that's half the size of me, and when they slip out, they're known to bond with the person closest to them. In earlier days, this was their parent, but now all eligible males and females travel to the Ember Clan to be there during the hatching. We remain there long enough for the vox to grow large enough to take flight, feeding and grooming it so it knows our touch. We learn to fly along with them, then take them to our homes so they know where to find us. They nest near us but always return to the Ember territory when they're ready to produce young, though that's only every three years."

"Fascinating."

Again, she wasn't frightened. This female stood up to the ashenclaws with only a stick. She rode my vox without fear. And she'd met my stare with a steely one of her own.

She was worthy of being my mate.

Was I worthy of her?

CHAPTER 7

ELERI

We flew through the night, and Odik guided his vox down to a meadow as dawn bloomed on the horizon.

I wasn't sure what I thought about being chosen by his clan. Could the fates send a pendant to give people guidance? Who was I to say? Somehow, the fates had sent me Zur when I was a child about to be eaten by shaydes.

A sob bubbled in my throat, but I swallowed it back down. Now wasn't the time to weep for my lost father. I'd do so when no one could see—and judge—me, though I wasn't sure Odik would laugh. He came across as stoic, serious, and full of compassion. I supposed he'd have to be to lead his clan from such an early age.

He'd lost his father, which meant he understood my feelings.

And we were now mated.

I'd never thought someone would choose to marry

me, not with my limp, so I wasn't sure what to think about having a husband. Everyone in the village had scorned me.

Yet Odik didn't reject me, or he hadn't so far. Perhaps my limp wasn't such a big thing to him. He'd calmly accepted my deficit, shrugging it off as if it was something to deal with but not something that would hold either of us back.

This . . . pleased me.

I wouldn't remain with him out of gratitude, however. I would wait to read his true character. If I continued to feel he was a good male, I'd stay with him. Returning to the village wasn't an option, and I needed to live somewhere.

Would I come to love him?

My fellow villagers would scorn me if they heard I was contemplating caring for an orc, but I'd never allowed anyone else's opinion of me matter, and I wouldn't in this.

Zarran landed in the meadow, and Odik leaped to the ground. He reached up and tugged me off the spine, then held me when my legs threatened to give way.

"I feel like they're permanently bowed wide," I said with a low laugh. My thighs spasmed, and my bad leg ached, though that wasn't anything new.

"I'll massage your legs later if you want." His voice came out deep and husky, and there was no missing the appreciative gaze he slid down my body. It made my skin flame and that secret place between my legs throb. No one had touched me there other than myself.

What would it be like to feel Odik's hand there? Would he know what to do or would he just rut when I told him it was alright for him to do so?

No, he'd just offered to massage my legs. If he didn't want to touch me in general, he wouldn't have made the suggestion.

"That would be nice of you," I said, striving to sound neutral and not needy. I wasn't a tiny, pet chall in desperate need of petting.

He gave me a curt nod. "Let me set up our camp, and then I'll do this for you."

I peered around at the surrounding forest, sucking in the cool air drifting out from the shadowy recesses. He'd told me the Malis Clan lived here, though I didn't see any sign of people. The forest was huge, however, and they could live in a different section.

How could a clan live where the shaydes hunted?

My skin peppered over with gooseflesh at the thought of never having a safe place to hide. The fortress walls penned us inside as much as they gave us protection, but at least there, I could sleep at night without worrying about an attack.

An attack from the shaydes, that is.

Birgid was just as vicious. Would I ever find vengeance for what she'd done? Perhaps one day, I'd make it happen.

"I'll build a fire," Odik said. "That'll keep the ashen-claws and shaydes away, though both usually hunt only at night."

"We're fortunate that we can fly above them."

"Indeed." As Odik strode over to the woods and collected downed branches, I hobbled after him, my legs twitching and my spine on fire with pain. How could orcs ride voxes without being as sore as me? Practice, most likely.

I collected sticks for kindling, bringing an armload over to where he carved out a small pit with the thick blade on the end of his staff. He'd carried that in a sheath on his back, and like with riding voxes, I bet that also took practice. Otherwise, he'd slice off someone's head if he turned too quickly. Or poke his own shoulder while sheathing it.

He crouched by the pit and carefully stacked the twigs I'd collected, adding thicker ones, then heavy branches. With a tindering stick, he soon had a merry blaze going. The day would warm up and it might be hot near the fire but knowing it would keep creatures away made me savor the heat.

"Sit." He removed a bundle wrapped in waxed cloth from a pouch and unwrapped it while I carefully lowered myself to the ground next to him.

It was heaven to stretch out my legs and wiggle my toes I'd stuffed into my shoes.

He broke a lump of seeds, nuts, and dried berries and handed me one of the pieces. "It's not much, but it'll satisfy your belly."

"Thank you." I took a big bite, savoring the mildly sweet flavors competing with the salty seeds.

He tugged a water flask from the pouch and offered it to me as well. It also held a hint of saltiness, but it went

down as easily as the meal. Hunger gave me an incredible appetite.

"Will I meet other human women?" I asked as we
continued eating. I shifted my legs, struggling to find a
position where they wouldn't ache. No real chance of
that.

"Eventually."

"What does that mean?"

"As I said, the Zephyr Clan lives far out to sea. You'll
be the first human woman to live there."

"I'm looking forward to seeing it." I struggled to keep
the wistful tone out of my voice. I couldn't pin all my
secret hopes for a home and family on Odik. He may
never do more than tolerate my presence. The idea of
anyone loving me outside of Zur was a strange concept.

Odik would plant orclings within my body once I told
him I was ready. I could only hope he treated me kindly.

Funny how I could almost picture him looking at me
with more than kindness.

Was I foolish to hope for his love?

ODIK

"You're uncomfortable," I said. She kept shifting her position, and while I sensed she tried to mask it, she winced whenever she moved.

It wasn't hard to remember how stiff and sore I was after my first ride on Zarran.

She curled her shoulders forward. "I'm sorry."

"Why?"

"Because it's never good to admit weakness."

That astonished me. "You've never ridden on a vox, have you?"

She shook her head.

"And you rode all night. I couldn't walk after my first ride, and that was only for a few hours." I curled my finger her way. "Come. Lie down and lift your skirt, mate."

Her shocked gaze met mine, and I chuckled at her assumption.

"Didn't I tell you I wouldn't claim you until you were

ready?" I said. "As I offered earlier, I want to massage your legs. Nothing else."

"I'm sorry. I guess I don't trust easily."

"And I haven't given you many reasons to believe you can trust me, but I hope you can somehow see the good in my heart and know I'm going to protect and cherish you always."

"Why?"

"Because you're my mate."

Her lips pursed. "Per your clan. I doubt you'd choose me on your own."

Why was her voice filled with such self-loathing? "Maybe I would if we'd met under normal circumstances. You're pretty."

"Caring takes time to develop and has nothing to do with how a person looks on the outside."

I liked hearing the spunk in her voice. She'd been calm and relaxed with me, and while it was nice that she wasn't fighting me, I worried that despite the strength she'd shown last night, she might not be strong enough for the harsh life we'd lead on the island. I wasn't so worried about that now.

"Back in the forest when the ashenclaws attacked, I saw more than your surface," I said. "I saw a woman who was willing to protect and bind my wounds. Who would've done her best not only to protect herself but also me. So don't think I only note your gorgeous hair that reminds me of the prettiest sunsets, or the color of your eyes, let alone your delectable, lush shape."

Her snort rang out. "I'm anything but gorgeous or delectable though I appreciate your kind words."

"I spoke from my heart, not to be kind. You don't see yourself as I do."

She tilted her head. "I don't understand you. The words you speak, yes, but I guess I don't know why you're being so nice to me, why you appear to *want* me."

"Has no one told you that you're special?"

"One person did," she said with a sad smile. Her eyes sparkled with tears. "You should know that I volunteered to be an orc bride. I wasn't forced into this like all the others. I took someone else's place. The man who raised me . . ." Her words choked off and tears trickled down her flushed cheeks. "He was murdered, and everyone accused me of doing it."

"Did you?"

"Of course not. I loved him."

"Would you like me to go back and slay them all for their false accusations?"

Her breath caught. "You can't do anything like that."

"I'm the Zephyr Clan caedos. Some might suggest I can do whatever I please."

"Not slay a bunch of people."

"I'd do it in your honor," I said softly.

She swallowed hard and rubbed my arm, her touch sending heat flaring through me. It centered in my cock, which was going to have to deal with deprivation for some time still.

"Thank you," she said. "But I'd rather you didn't. One of them deserves death but let her wallow in the guilt she'll carry for the rest of her days. That'll punish her more than the crack of your staff against her head. That would end it much too soon."

"Say the word, mate," I said, my voice gone husky. "I vow I'll do anything to make you happy."

"You don't need to." Her steely gaze met mine. "One day, though I don't know how it will be possible, vengeance will be mine."

Yes, she did have the strength she'd need to take on the challenges we'd face living on the island.

She was beautiful. No one would state anything differently. But I did see more than her outer surface.

I saw a woman I could easily love.

CHAPTER 9
ELERI

In a very short time, I'd learned orcs were nothing like what my villagers whispered about with horror tainting their words. Odik was no monster, no savage creature, though I'd already seen how amazing he was in battle. I suspected he could fight off almost anything, and some might consider that savage.

Inside, he truly was a kind person.

My fellow villagers had done the orcs a grave disservice.

I laid on the ground and tentatively lifted my skirt up to my mid-thighs, watching him with my breath hitching in and out of me. I wasn't frightened. No, I was intrigued.

Maybe I was a foolish woman succumbing to the first male to treat me nicely. I'd drown in what he offered while he'd walk away after, completely unaware of how enthralled I'd become with him.

Although, Odik didn't appear to be that kind of

person. I didn't know how I could be so sure about this, but I was. He called me his mate, and he meant it.

He'd talked with me, seen how I walked, and he still wanted to *claim* me.

Odik stared at my legs for so long, I worried he was suddenly seeing my flaws and judging them as being unworthy of mating with such a fierce and handsome orc. With a curt nod I couldn't interpret, he moved closer to me, stopping beside my knees.

When he laid his hands on my lower legs, I gasped.

"Pain?" he asked, lifting his hands off me.

"No."

A frown flickered across his face, but he said nothing, starting again with his warm, calloused palms and fingertips gently rubbing from my knee to the top of my foot. I wore nothing beneath my skirt but my underwear, which meant my legs were bare.

He lifted my right heel onto his thighs and stared at the network of scars traveling from above my thigh all the way to my ankle. "This must've hurt horribly."

"I was three when it happened. Only in my dreams do I seem to remember, but when I wake to my cries, I still can't picture anything but the endless pain."

"I'm sorry. Sometimes we block out the worst things in life to protect our souls."

"Is that what you think I've done?"

He shrugged and gently worked on my calf. I groaned at how amazing his touch felt.

"You're skilled with your hands," I said.

He shot me a grin, and I marveled that I could find

tusks and a coarse orc face so appealing. "I can't say I've had practice. You're small and delicate. I'm frightened I'll hurt you."

"I don't believe you can." I couldn't tell how I knew this already, but something was growing between us, something precious I wanted to treasure.

Could I be falling in love already?

That would be a mistake on my part. Odik was a good person. He'd never knowingly harm me. But like everyone else other than Zur, I doubted he'd find a way to love me. Look what Birgid had done! She'd murdered the only person who cared for me solely to drive me from the village.

I was too damaged for anyone to care for.

Odik finished with my right leg and went around to the other side to work on my left. Each stroke of his fingers sent tingles across my skin. I liked it when he touched me.

Too much.

As he worked on the tightness in my thighs, heat spiraled inside me. I wasn't sure how to interpret the feeling, but I sensed it was lust. His fingers felt good; it was natural for me to think of him placing them in more intimate areas.

Wetness pooled between my legs, and I shifted on the ground, suddenly wanting more.

He lifted his head as if he was scenting the air before his golden gaze pinned me in place. After easing my legs off his lap, he put an arm's length between us. "We need to sleep now."

"Alright." I felt limpid yet excited at the same time, though I didn't know why I was excited.

"Lay by the fire," he said curtly. "I'll patrol the area and will wake you at dusk."

I didn't know why he was irritated with me, but I wasn't going to ask. With a nod, I curled up near the fire.

Sleep did not come quickly.

CHAPTER 10

ELERI

Odik woke me as the sun was starting to set.

"We ride," was all he said as he helped me rise to my feet.

When my legs nearly gave way, he swept me up in his arms and carried me with quick strides over to Zarran. One leap, and we were both mounted on the vox's spine. A nudge of his heels, and the beast took flight, soaring over the forest toward our destination.

We flew through the night.

"Tell me more about the island you call home," I asked. "You said the surface is well above the water?"

"Steep cliffs surround the upper surface with no easy access for dresalods."

"You mentioned them before. What are they?"

"A sea creature as fierce as the shaydes," he said grimly.

He guided Zarran to the right to avoid a large flock of birds. Some spied the vox and squawked, diving toward the forest with the rest flapping furiously behind. They disappeared into the vegetation.

"Dresalods live deep below the sea. They're as big as orcs and have spikes on each of their six limbs, plus large claws on the front of their hard exoskeleton. They use those to climb and battle."

"They sound fearsome," I said with a shiver, unable to imagine a beast such as this.

"The cliffs deter them, though they do occasionally attack. They savor our flesh."

My shivers turned to full-on trembles.

Odik's arms tightened around me. "I'll protect you from them."

But what would protect him from them?

"They attack often?" I asked with a thready voice. I didn't fear much, but the idea of sea creatures the size of orcs attacking us almost made me eager to return to the forest and face the shaydes and ashenclaws. At least I understood them. I knew almost nothing about the dresalods.

"They rarely bother with the islands. The topography provides too much of a challenge. And they only attack at night and infrequently."

"*How* often?" If this was going to be my home, I needed to know.

He shrugged. "Every six months or so, when their numbers have grown enough to make them feel brave. Never fear, though. We hear them coming long before they arrive. They tend to shriek as they leave the sea. We pull up our steps, making it harder for them to climb, then drop boulders down on them when they try to scale the stone surface. Few make it to the top, and they're quickly dispatched."

"It doesn't make me eager to go near the sea.

"I'll keep you safe."

I had to trust him. After all, he'd lived this long with the creatures. He must be quite savvy when it comes to dresalods.

"What else can you tell me about the island?"

"It's the largest in a chain of islands, and orcs only live on the main bit of land. The others are too small to support our way of life for long. As for the island itself, it's made up of open areas and some forest. We grow our own crops, and we have a tight, friendly community. The island itself is prettier than any place you've ever seen." Pride and happiness shone in his voice. "I love it there. I can't imagine living anywhere else. You'll enjoy it there too."

Other than the dresalods, I suspected I would. But I could keep watch like the orcs did. And over time, I would learn how to fight them too. Not as well as an orc. I was nowhere near as strong.

But my strength came from inside, where it most mattered.

We flew until morning came again, and Odik landed Zarran in another small meadow.

Like before, I hobbled behind Odik collecting sticks for the fire, struggling not to groan. I ached so much I winced with each step. I wasn't sure there was a muscle left in my body that didn't spasm.

He refilled the flask at a snaky stream winding through the woods near the meadow.

"You can wash here if you'd like."

The water might be cold, but the idea sounded heavenly. With my bag of clothing in hand, I limped over to the water.

As much as I wanted to strip and sit in the stream, I wasn't confident about removing my clothing around Odik. I wasn't worried he'd attack me. He'd already proven he was a good person.

But my skin tingled whenever I thought of him studying my naked body. I wasn't exactly sure what the tingling meant, but I suspected it was related to the attraction I was beginning to feel for the strong orc who called me his mate.

Removing my undergarment, I washed it and laid it on a flat rock to dry in the sun. I stood in the water with my legs spread and cleaned up as best as I could.

"I'll turn away if it makes you feel more comfortable," he called out from where he crouched beside the newly laid fire. He tossed a stick into the flames and didn't look my way.

Alright. I needed to feel clean.

With my back to him, I removed my blouse, washed it out and laid it in the sun beside the undergarment. I stripped off my skirt and, naked, sat in the water that only came to my waist. I couldn't hold back a yip. Damn, it was cold!

Odik's gaze cut my way before he whipped his head back to face the fire.

"You're not harmed?" he called out.

"No. Sorry. The water's cold. But it feels great." I washed myself and even laid back and did my hair as best I could. Too bad they hadn't included soap in the bag they gave each woman leaving the fortress for the hunt.

"I'll bathe after you," he said.

Rising from the water, I used my blouse to blot off most of the water. I wrung out my hair and braided it to keep it from soaking through my clean clothing and dressed quickly.

My teeth chattered as I hurried to the fire, but I felt decent for the first time in days.

"Keep an eye on Zarran," Odik said, rising. "He'll alert you if he hears any threat. Call out to me."

"I will." I sat near the fire, stretching my twitching fingers toward it to suck in the heat.

"There's food in the bag. Feel welcome to eat." He grabbed clothing and strode toward the river.

I fully intended to grant him the same privacy he gave me, but I couldn't help it. Curiosity might be my downfall, but I peeked through my lashes as he tugged off his clothing and stepped into the water.

I didn't see much, just the shadow of his cock and his nicely shaped butt. He was greenish gold all over, and the sun seemed to stroke his skin, making it gleam.

More tingles spread through me, confirming my earlier suspicion. I was attracted to my new orc husband, and I wasn't sure what—if anything—I should do about it.

There was one thing I *could* do. I completely turned away from the stream and faced the fire. I didn't look Odik's way until he was fully dressed and walking back toward me.

"You're sore again," he said after we'd finished eating. "Let me massage your back and legs." He patted his lap.

Should I refuse him? His touch had sparked something inside me I wasn't sure I wanted to explore again. Not when I was already attracted to him. But he'd eventually be my full husband, a thought that didn't frighten me any longer.

He patted his lap again. "Eleri."

Nodding, I rose, and he tugged me down onto his lap facing away from him. His fingers gently worked down my back, stroking at first, then deepening his touch. He worked out each kink and seemed to know exactly where I was sore the most.

In no time, I was melting, struggling not to moan where I sat in his lap. Heat pooled between my legs, and even for a virgin, I was savvy enough to know what that meant.

He eased me onto my back beside him and rubbed one of my legs, then the other, moving his fingers carefully and with just enough pressure to make me melt some more.

"I've never been with a male," I blurted out as he finished kneading my right thigh.

"Why not?"

"Because no one wanted me." Maybe Birgid's

husband who'd winked that one time would've taken me if I'd offered.

Or maybe he hadn't winked. He'd had something in his eye.

"That, I cannot believe," Odik said.

"You're too kind."

"I'm being honest. I want you." His voice sounded hollow. His gaze glided across my body like a caress, and more heat slicked through me, centering in my core.

"Have you ever touched yourself?" he asked.

"What?" I barked, starting to sit up.

He gently pressed me back to the ground. "I asked if you've ever touched yourself." His eyes landed on that place between my legs that throbbed.

I shifted on the grass, flushed and overcome with a need I'd never felt before.

"It's all right if you haven't," he said. "Always be honest with me, and I'll do the same with you."

"I *have* touched myself." The words jerked out of me. I was deficient enough already without coming across as completely inexperienced. "A few times."

His head tilted, and a smile flitted across his lips before he smoothed them. "Would you do it right now?"

I sucked in a breath.

Heat smoldered in his eyes. "I want you to show me what your body enjoys, Eleri."

CHAPTER 11

ODIK

I could smell the faint essence of her heated musk before I started massaging her right thigh, and it made my cock roar with approval.

My pendant glowed, nearly blinding in its intensity.

She may not wish to be mated with an orc, she may not find me attractive, but it was clear that I stirred something inside her.

I could work with it.

Her virginity didn't matter. Well, it did. Knowing I'd be her first made me want to puff my chest and roar, a completely stupid feeling. It shouldn't matter if she was experienced or not. I wanted her. That was all that mattered.

"You want me to touch myself?" she asked in shock.

"Yes. Show me how you pleasure your body."

"I . . ." She pinched her eyelids shut and when they opened again, a hint of lust lingered there.

I could work with that too.

"You don't have to if you don't want to," I said, continuing to make smooth circles on her thighs, slowly working my hands higher. She may not have realized it, but as I rubbed her legs, she kept moving them apart.

"It feels weird to think of doing that while you watch," she gulped out.

"I could look away while you do it. You could . . . describe what you're doing. That would be enough."

Her laugh hitched in her throat, cut off too soon. "I thought the whole point of me pleasuring myself was for you to watch."

There wasn't much I wouldn't do to be given such a chance. "I don't want you to feel uncomfortable."

She dragged in a breath and whooshed it out, sending a few stray wisps of her glorious hair flipping up into the air before it settled with the rest. I couldn't look away from its lovely length. It was all I could do not to unbraid it and bury my face in the strands.

"You could close your eyes," I said. "Pretend I'm not here."

"You won't . . . attack me or anything, will you? I mean, if I expose myself."

"I've told you I won't touch you until you want it." And I was going to do everything I could to make sure she wanted it, and soon. I'd felt her gaze linger on me, and it wasn't with derision. Like I couldn't look away from her, she had the same absorption as me.

She was my mate. This was how it was supposed to be, but it still thrilled through me, making my cock surge up even further. I couldn't wait for the time she curled her finger my way, urging me to climb all over her. Bury myself deeply inside her body.

"Alright." Her skin quivered, and her giddy laugh slipped out. "I can't believe I'm doing this." With a quick tug, she lifted her skirt up to her waist, exposing the garment she wore beneath. "The few times I've touched myself, I first made sure I was alone. It would be embarrassing for anyone to see something like this."

"I'm your mate. There's nothing embarrassing about showing me how to please you, let alone to expose your body to me."

"We only recently met."

"We'll eventually know each other intimately."

"I guess you're right." With one last long look at me, she hitched down her undergarment, and her slickness gleamed in the morning light.

I groaned and her gaze met mine, containing a knowing that some females seemed to be born with. She understood that I wanted her. That I *craved* her. I'd never deny it.

What I wouldn't give to lick her between the legs, to suck on her clit and keep doing it until she shouted her pleasure.

Soon.

"*I'm* going to close my eyes," she said. "You're looking at me like you want to consume me."

"I wouldn't be Odik if I didn't." Yes, I'd consume her, though not today. Perhaps I'd take a bit longer to reach our home. I could afford an extra day. By then, she might even let me touch her.

"Show me what makes you feel good," I said, stroking her thighs. I was so close to her, I could see everything from her engorged clit to the wetness dripping from her tight passage.

"Don't talk," she barked. "If you do, I'm going to remember you're here, and then I won't be able to fully relax."

"Alright." I'd never speak again as long as her fingers didn't stop wandering down across her belly.

She lifted her knees and parted her thighs, and I clenched my jaw tight to keep from groaning. Her fingertips teased across the top of her thigh. When she parted her folds and placed one on her clit, my cock smacked against my abs.

"You should pleasure yourself," she said, her voice containing a huskiness that shot straight through me. "Then you won't have to run around with a staff in your pants."

"How do you know I'm aroused?"

"It could be an assumption on my part, but I know men even if I haven't been intimate with them. There's no one back at the village I could do this with who wouldn't become stiff."

"You're right. I'm completely enthralled by you, mate. All I can think of is sinking my cock into your hot, wet passage, of driving hard while stroking your clit until you shatter."

"You're talking."

My grin slipped out. "I apologize. I'll stop."

"Focus on your cock, and I'll do . . . this." She slipped

a fingertip from her other hand inside her wetness. While rubbing her clit, she pumped the finger in and out. Her breathing picked up, and I didn't have to touch my cock for it to explode.

Releasing it from my loincloth, I clutched it.

"You're incredibly wet," I growled. The slurping sound her finger made was driving me out of my mind. "You like pumping your finger. Try two."

Her finger stopped. "I haven't done that before."

"See if you like it. If not, you can back off to one again."

"Ah, yes." Another finger joined the first, moving deep inside her while her other hand tended to her clit. "It feels even better."

"Try three," I growled.

"Are you stroking yourself?"

If I did, I'd come. I wanted to hold back, to do it when she did even if I wasn't buried within her at the time. "Three fingers."

A smile flitted across her face before it smoothed once more. She pumped three fingers inside her tight little passage. "This feels good. I like the thickness. Funny how I didn't think of this before."

"My cock is thicker and longer than your fingers."

"And I know where you want to put it. Stroke yourself!"

"Very well, mate. At your command."

While I pumped my engorged cock, she continued to lazily glide her fingers in and out of her channel while rolling her clit.

"Can I use some of your wetness?" I asked.

A frown crossed her pretty face. "For what?"

"If I rub myself too hard, I could get a rash."

"Well, then don't rub it too hard."

"If I don't, I'll continue to have as you said, a staff in my pants."

"You can use some of my wetness, since I appear to be generating a lot of it, but don't do anything you shouldn't."

I was going to die if I didn't get to touch her. "I'll just . . ." Leaning close to her, I slid my finger in with hers. So tight. So wet. My cock jerked upward, very close to blasting.

Her breath caught, and she pumped her hips up as I shifted my finger, making sure to stroke her inner walls. I pulled it out and slide it down my cock, nearly exploding, before sliding it back inside her.

"I could do this part for you if you want," I said. "My fingers are thicker."

"How will you take care of yourself while doing that?"

"You don't need to worry about me. Just relax and feel. Tell me if this hurts or not." I nudged aside her hand and drove two fingers inside her.

"Ah," she gasped.

"Pain?"

"No, it feels good."

Fuck. My precious mate was going to be the death of me.

My balls surged upward and fire scorched through

my veins as I continued to push my fingers inside her and pull them back out. She could handle three, which was good because I was even thicker.

"That feels amazing. Don't stop." While she rubbed her clit, I finger-fucked my new bride.

And when she exploded, her moan rippling across the small meadow, I joined her, shooting my seed in thick spurts toward the fire.

ELERI

Should I be embarrassed by what we'd just done together? I hadn't known Odik for long. We'd shared some of our pasts, but we hadn't learned much about each other. We hadn't even kissed!

What he'd done had felt so decadent. Like I'd stepped out of the staid village and into the arms of someone who turned me into a wanton creature.

I wanted him to do it again.

Instead of suggesting he keep moving his fingers inside me, I urged his hand away, fixed my clothing, and sat up. I scooted away from him for good measure.

He took my cue and fixed his own clothing, then fiddled with the fire. Gathering what we hadn't eaten, he tucked it inside the pouch.

I was grateful he didn't mention what happened.

"We'll sleep as much as we can today, then continue traveling," he said, patting the ground beside him. "You need to lie here with me."

"Because we're getting married?"

"According to my people and traditions, we're already married. Orcs call it mated. My pendant choosing you, followed by me tracking you down in the forest and capturing you, was the only ceremony needed to link us together for the rest of our lives."

A silly thrill shot through me. I didn't want him to feel obligated to be with me solely because his pendant took an inopportune moment to flare when I was around, but I was uncomfortably attracted to him. I'd hate to think he'd tell me to find someplace else to live when we reached his island home.

"You didn't exactly capture me," I pointed out.

His mouth quirked up in one corner. "We can loosely call it that."

"You collapsed at my feet."

"Something I'm completely embarrassed about."

"Why? You'd taken blows to the head. You passed out—"

"Something else I'm profoundly embarrassed about."

"It's natural. It happens at times like that. It's nothing to be concerned about."

"It doesn't happen to me," he grumbled.

When I grinned, his smile bloomed fully, and we both started laughing.

"Truly, you don't need to be worried about it," I said.

His mood sobered. "Truly, you need to come lay down beside me."

"The fire's just as warm on the opposite side."

"Your back needs to face me. Then if something attacks, it'll go for me first."

"Won't you or Zarran hear something coming?"

"I'd be mortified if I didn't." His sharp gaze met mine. "I'll kill anything and anyone that touches you."

"What if it's a cute little creature like a chall?" I was teasing—*testing* him—though I wasn't sure why.

Actually, I knew why. I was worried if I laid beside him, his fingers would wander, I'd spread my legs, and the next thing I knew, we'd be rutting. I knew it was coming, but I felt depraved for craving him so soon after meeting him. Surely I needed to know him a bit more before we progressed to something like that?

"If it's a cute little creature like a chall, I promise not to kill it." His stern gaze met mine. "Come lay beside me, mate. I've told you I won't do anything you don't want me to."

And that was the problem. I was beginning to think I'd enjoy *everything* he chose to do with me.

However, it was childish to sit across the fire from him, arguing about me doing something as normal as lying with him for protection.

I rose and walked around to join him, resting on my side, facing the fire.

He settled behind me, his arms going around me, reminding me again of how much bigger than me he was when he could rest his chin on the top of my head with his knees lying by my feet. At least this kept his cock well beyond intimate areas if it came seeking.

"In all honesty," I whispered. "I peeked."

"At what?" The soft murmur of his voice was incredibly soothing. It lulled me, just like *he* lulled me.

"Your cock."

"And what are your thoughts about my cock?"

"It's big."

"So am I," he grumbled, following it up with a yawn.

"I'm keeping you awake. I'm sorry." Heat scorched my face, and it didn't come from the crackling fire.

"It's not a problem. Do share your thoughts about my cock."

"Why?" I asked.

"Call it curiosity on my part."

"It's also thick and veiny."

"The veins keep the blood flowing, something I think you'll agree is important," he said gruffly.

"Naturally. It also has nubs on the sides."

"They vibrate when I'm aroused."

I'd missed that, but how intriguing. "What do they feel like inside a woman?"

"You'd need to ask a woman to hear the answer to that question."

My belly burned with jealousy, and I wanted to gnash my teeth. "*Who* has discovered this?" I bit out carefully.

He chuckled. "No need to be worried, sweet thing. My nubs exist solely for you."

"You've given them to someone else or you wouldn't know what they do."

"Today is not the first time I've touched my cock."

"Well, of course," I said primly. Lifting a pebble, I

threw it into the fire, which ignored my childish gesture. "Today wasn't the first time I've touched my body either."

"Of course." He mimicked me—*mocked me.*

"I'm not jealous."

"You have no reason to be. From now on, I promise not to share my nubs with anyone but you."

"Not even your hand?" I asked.

"Now, that's an interesting question. I guess the answer will depend on what happens over the next few days."

"What do you think's going to happen over the next few days?"

"I believe, my sweet mate, you'll have to wait to find out."

I rolled my eyes, though I didn't argue his point. At the rate we were going, I'd be humping him by the end of the day.

"You also have a second cock," I said.

"You're quite an observant mate, aren't you?"

"I educate myself."

He released a deep chuckle. "Educate yourself about cocks?"

"Only yours. So far."

"Always only mine," he growled.

"Possessive, aren't you?" The thought made the blood hum through my veins.

"I don't share. You're mine, and you'll soon become used to the notion."

I wanted to protest that I belonged to no one, but I

suspected he was right. "If I'm yours, then that means you're mine." I said it smugly.

"Exactly." Pure satisfaction came through in his voice. "As for my second cock, it's called a spur."

"Does it vibrate too?" I was getting wet between my legs again, which was silly. I'd never needed to pleasure myself more than once or twice a month. Certainly not two times within the span of a few moments.

"It will latch onto your pretty little clit and suck it while I pump my cock—complete with vibrating nubs—inside you."

I was quivering at the idea. Lust was roaring through me, and I wasn't sure what I should do about it. Nothing, I supposed. It wasn't like I was going to ask him to push his fingers inside me again.

Though I wanted to.

CHAPTER 13
ODIK

I was grateful when Eleri slept. If she kept talking about my cock and wiggling while making those little huffing sounds she'd released while I was pumping my fingers inside her, I was going to explode.

Again.

Or tease her into letting me strip off her clothing. If she thought my fingers were skilled, wait until she felt my tongue. I'd suck on her clit while stroking her slick inner walls.

Fuck.

My cock was on fire all over again because of my sweet mate. I'd thank the fates each day of my life for gifting her to me.

While she slumbered in my arms, I dozed. I'd be foolish to sleep deeply, but I needed the rest as much as she did.

I woke before her as the sun was slanting its way across the sky, heading for its bed for the night. Easing away from her, I rose to a crouch, peering around the clearing.

Zarran resting calmly on his haunches told me nothing dangerous crept nearby. Voxes had uncanny hearing, and he'd snort or bellow if he sensed an attack.

It was a good "night," all things considered. While we'd decimated the shayde population as repayment for killing most of our females, a few lingered. They bred, and their population was growing once more. There was enough now to make trouble, and enough that the humans still needed our protection in exchange for gifting us with two females once a year.

It was going to take many generations to birth enough orclings to replace our loss, and that was just numbers. We'd never replace them in our hearts.

I added more wood to the fire, though we didn't need it for heat. Now that I was fully awake, we didn't need it for protection either. The light was cheery, and I liked it, and that was good enough for me.

After walking the perimeter of the meadow and listening, but hearing nothing of concern in the forest, I went over to Zarran. I patted him, which he loved, plus gave a rubdown with a thick cloth, which he adored. He gruffed and sighed while I worked on his shoulders, adding extra rubs to work out any muscle kinks. He'd flown two nights to reach the village and now I was asking him to fly some more. If I didn't take good care of him, he couldn't give his all to protect me.

And if the dresalods attacked once we reached the

island, which they did more often than I liked, he wouldn't be in prime shape to help me fight them.

After I finished and gave him more pats to his cheeks, I turned to find Eleri sitting up, re-braiding her long hair the color of a sunset. I'd never seen anything that color outside of blossoms. Orcs universally had black hair, though some clans had shades of burgundy or green among the strands.

Her hair was long, thick, and skimmed across her lush ass. I'll admit I spent part of the night scooted low behind her so I could sniff the floral-scented strands.

"Can I go to the woods?" she asked when she'd finished plaiting her hair. She wound it up onto the top of her head, creating a crown that suited her new role as a leader's mate.

What would my people think of her? She'd be the first human to come to the island, and I worried they wouldn't make her feel welcome. Although few would scorn her now that our females were nearly all dead. Anyone who was willing to bear our orclings would be treasured.

"Of course." With my thick staff in hand, I followed her just inside the woods. I turned and scanned the area while she took care of her needs.

"I don't suppose there's water for washing?" she asked when we returned to the meadow.

"Only what we need to drink. We'll fly part of the night but stop where I can refill the flask. You can swim there if you'd like." And I could ogle her body if she didn't ask me to turn away.

"I've never swam before."

"You bathe." She smelled sweet, not of sweat.

"Back at the village, I washed up at the river; all of us do. But while others go in deeper, I never have."

"Why not?"

She smiled at me. "Maybe I worry about the fish nibbling on my toes."

"We swim in the sea surrounding my island home," I said.

"What's it like?"

I put out the fire and gathered our few things together, preparing to fly.

"Refreshing when it's hot in the summer. Icy when it's cold in the winter."

"Maybe you can teach me to swim."

"I'd be happy to." I could easily picture myself holding her in my arms while she clung to my shoulders. We'd be naked, of course, and she'd wrap her legs around my waist. I could take her to a big smooth rock on the shore, hoist her up, then follow, rising over her where I could stroke her water slick body.

My cock bobbed to attention once more.

I really needed to stop thinking about rutting with my mate until I could actually rut with her. Otherwise, I was going to walk around with an uncomfortable stick in my pants.

"You're vibrating," she said with a laugh.

"Excuse me?" I asked as I hooked the pouch with our food and water over one of Zarran's neck spikes. We could eat and drink as we flew.

"Your cock."

"You're quite observant."

"It's poking the front of your pants."

"Equally observant," I said with a laugh. For someone with no experience, she was refreshingly honest about sexual organs. And the way she'd touched herself early this morning . . .

It was going to take me a long time to get that out of my mind.

"Do you want to go into the woods and take care of it before we fly?" I asked, feeling mischievous. We'd found pleasure at the same time earlier, and for some reason, that made me feel as if I knew him intimately.

"I'd rather take care of it while pleasuring you," he said.

My skin flamed, heat scorching my cheeks.

"We don't know each other very well," I said.

"So says the woman who came apart from my fingers."

"I was aroused."

He grinned. "And I suspect you're getting aroused right now."

I stomped my foot, feeling foolish the moment I did it. "How can you know something like that?"

"I know you quite well now, mate."

"It's backward to start with sexual activities before

we know . . . say, our last names. Our favorite foods. Or if we'll even like each other." Though I liked him already. I thought I'd find myself with a coarse, snarly orc who'd fling me to the ground and claim my body. I'd live a dreary life, producing one child after another for him, until my heart gave out and I died.

That's what the whispered tales from my village said.

Reality was proving to be much different from the nightmares they spread.

"Brunellon is my last name," he said. "I love fish, and I'm not picky about how it's prepared."

"Why not?"

"Because I'm a horrible cook."

"I can cook. Quite well," I said smugly. Finally, I had something I could offer this orc who already seemed to have everything he needed.

"And I like you already." He crinkled the skin around his deep golden eyes, smiling. "Can we rut now?"

"Ha." I playfully slapped his arm.

He rewarded my impertinence by tossing me up onto Zarran's back and leaping to land behind me. He tugged me back until I half sat on his lap, and his big cock prodded my spine through his leather loincloth. I supposed he wore a garment like that so he could easily tug his cock out to rut.

Actually, I didn't want to think too hard about who he might've rutted with in the past.

I *wasn't* jealous.

A nudge of his heels, and Zarran sprang upward, his wings spiking out and flapping to catch the wind. In no time, we were soaring above the forest that stretched forever, and I was stretching my arms out once again to snag the breeze.

"I adore flying," I said, leaning into Odik's embrace.

"I adore you," he growled in my ear.

His cock had not subsided. And the thought of what he'd done with his fingers was making heat zip down my spine like a lightning bolt had arced from the sky.

His hands landed on my thighs and he massaged them. I was certain he was pretending to do this to keep me from cramping, but each time his fingertips stroked inward, they reached closer to the junction between my thighs.

"You might as well pull up my skirts and get it over with," I said, though without irritation. I felt flushed and overheated, and the thought of stripping off my clothing and jumping into a cool sea held great appeal.

As did rising up and seeing what it would feel like when his cock took the place his fingers had claimed this morning.

I couldn't imagine what had come over me.

"Sanderson. Fruit. And I like you too," I belted out.

He chuckled. "See? We know each other fairly well now."

We didn't, but as he slid my skirt up and slipped his hand down into my undergarment, expertly finding my clit, I didn't give a damn about that.

"Tell me what you like," he said by my ear. He rocked against me, his stiff cock humming. Truly, he was huge.

His fingers felt good, but they were smaller than that thing between his legs.

"You saw me touching my clit, and you would've seen more if you'd allowed me to finish on my own," I chided him, grinning so wide, my cheeks ached.

Zarran flew on, oblivious to what we were doing, thank the fates.

Odik kept rubbing my clit.

"I apologize. If you'd like to do this yourself, I'll be happy to back off and leave you to it." He tugged his hand out of my undergarment, but it didn't get far before I grabbed it and returned it to where it belonged.

Belonged? Boy, was I quickly giving in to his charm.

"Show me how *you'd* pleasure me," I said.

"I already did."

"Once might not have been enough."

"I like that you're so open about this, sweet mate," he said, still shifting his cock against my back.

"Won't the rubbing give you a rash?" I asked, remembering his words last night.

"It'll be worth it."

I didn't feel sexually brave enough to suggest he wouldn't get a rash if he rocked it inside me.

Despite our teasing about knowing—and liking—each other, I felt I should hold off at least until we reached his home. *Our* home, I supposed, since I'd live there with him.

He stroked down my slit, groaning. "Damn, you're wet."

"I've heard that's a good thing. I will clarify that I've

overheard this. I didn't have many friends in the village, so they weren't chatting with me about stuff like this, though they didn't hold back their words when I was around."

You'd think I could say something that would make me sound likeable instead of the village reject.

Thankfully, he didn't latch onto my embarrassing slip. "It's a very good thing. I'll make sure you're very wet before I give you my cock."

He slid a few fingers inside me while his thumb paid exquisite attention to my clit.

My moan wretched out, and Zarran appeared to pause in flight, peering around.

My cheeks overheated once more, but at least the beast didn't realize I was the one making the sound.

"Later, I'm going to do this with my mouth," Odik said softly while pumping his fingers in and out of my passage.

"How can anyone do this with their mouth?" I could barely focus on speaking. "Your tongue's not as long as your fingers."

"You'll be pleasantly surprised."

He continued to finger fuck me while I rose and dropped down hard on his hand. I was so close; it wouldn't take me much more to spill over. I marveled that he could figure out what pleased me so quickly. It had taken me more than a month to understand my body and bring myself to orgasm the first time.

Moaning, I bucked against Odik's hand. He rewarded me with increased pressure on my clit.

I was going to fall apart in seconds.

It crashed through me all of a sudden, and I shuddered in Odik's arms, my eyes pinching shut so I could block out everything but the pleasure he was giving me.

His cock remained hard, and I assumed it must throb, but I wasn't sure what to offer. There was no way we could do more while riding on Zarran even if I was ready.

Which, despite two incredible orgasms, I wasn't sure I was.

He pulled his fingers out of me and while I straightened my clothing, he licked my essence off his hand. I should be horrified that he was doing something like that, but all I could think of was his promise to place his mouth where his fingers had been.

We continued to fly through the night, talking about general stuff. Maybe we were both feeling overwhelmed by how quickly our relationship was developing.

I knew I was.

We passed through a gap in an enormous mountain range, and Zarran swooped down into a large valley. The sea glistened beyond.

"I've never seen a body of water that huge," I breathed. "We'll fly over it to reach your island, won't we?"

"We will." Pride shone in his voice, and it lifted with excitement. "We're nearly home."

I was both nervous and eager to see where I'd live. Would the other orcs treat me like the villagers had? Actually, as long as they behaved decently to me, it would be an improvement.

As the sun started slanting its way across the world, heralding dawn, we passed over a big city made up of buildings that gleamed silver so bright, it was nearly blinding.

"Gorgeous," I breathed. "It's amazing. So many buildings. Orcs, I assume, too."

"Yes, many. My friend, Jaus, lives here, as does the royal family, though they spend their summers in their seaside palace and their winters in the mountains. About one thousand people live in the city. Others were built along the sea to the north and south. My clan is the only one that lives far out to sea."

"It must be wonderful to live in such a place as this."

Zarran flew over an enormous wall rising between the city and shore, and guards with numerous weapons looked up and waved.

"Why so many guards?"

"They watch for dresalods."

I shrunk in Odik's arms, though I was clearly safer here than I would be on land. "I don't see any attacking."

"It's a good day, then." His grim tone sunk all the way to my bones.

My skin crawled with fear. Soon, we'd reach the island, and we'd no longer be in flight. I'd started to look forward to living with Odik, but now I wasn't sure.

This world was much bigger—and more dangerous —than I'd ever realized.

CHAPTER 15

ODIK

We left the city behind and flew over the sea.

"Where are the islands?"

"We'll fly for a bit longer before we see them."

"They're far from the city, then. And you said you grow your own food."

How could I tell her we got by as best we could, that we were a people struggling to survive? We had incredible wealth and not only in the joy we took from living on the island, but from the precious stones we mined in the sea around us and within the land itself. But the one thing we needed; we couldn't buy.

"I hope you'll be happy with us," I said instead of what I should. She'd see and for these final moments, I wanted to hold her and drink in the optimism that rose from her smooth skin. All too soon, I'd have to rip off the sheen and expose her to what the rest of us lived with.

"When I left the fortress, I said goodbye," she said. "I determined right then to only look forward."

"You're very brave."

"I'm resourceful. I've had to be all my life. Zur was good to me. He was the father I needed. And as he grew older, I took care of him like he had me. But he's gone now." Her voice hollowed out with pain. "How could she do that to him? He was good and kind, and he never caused anyone harm." Her body shook as she wept, but she remained silent even in this, as if she'd long since learned not to draw attention.

I tightened my arms around her and murmured soothing words, though I couldn't tell if they helped. She needed to mourn, and that was often a solitary thing. I'd done the same when I lost my parents during the shayde attack. Then, my people needed me to step in and take his place, not wallow in my sorrow.

"I'm sorry," she finally said.

"Why?"

"For crying. I should lift my chin and find the strength to live like Zur would've wanted."

"There's nothing wrong with giving in to your pain."

"Weeping serves no purpose." She said it with a thread of strength in her voice.

"Your words or . . .?"

"Zur held me when I was little, and I cried. I did that much too often. But no, he never told me I couldn't mourn. Others did, however, and their mean words sunk through my skin and latched onto my bones."

A growl ripped through me. "You're saying other children mocked you."

She tensed in my arms, and I wondered if she thought I'd someday reject her like almost everyone else. "Not just children."

I shook my head, but I knew enough adults who'd behave the same. Sadly, not everyone was eager to extend kindness to others. "Some people are foolish. They make assumptions based on someone's surface, never looking hard enough to see the core of the person inside." I rested my chin on the top of her head. "You're incredibly strong, Eleri. You'd have to be to survive what happened when you were small. Look at you, not allowing those in the village to convict you of a crime you didn't commit. You left, which was wise. That also took strength."

"I did what I had to."

"That's all we can ever do."

She was quiet a long moment, perhaps processing my words. "Do you ever cry?"

"I haven't for such a long time, I'm not sure I remember how."

"Why not?"

I shrugged. "I'm the caedos of my clan. I need to remain strong for them if not for myself."

"Zur told me all emotions are equally valid."

"He sounds like a wonderful male. I'm sorry I won't get to meet him."

"Me too." Her voice trembled, and I wished there was something I could do to ease her pain.

"My offer still stands. I'll be happy to slay the person who murdered your friend."

She was silent for a long time. "She knows what she did, and now she'll have to live with that knowledge for the rest of her days."

"If you change your mind—"

"I won't." She squeezed my arms where her hands rested on them. "Thank you. I never dreamed I'd ever meet someone like you when I fled the village."

"I prayed I'd meet someone like you." It wasn't weakness to admit something like that. "I'm strong for my people because I have to be. But when I'm in my home, it's nice to relax and be the orc I am inside."

"I see your strength and your kindness, Odik, and I like it very much."

And that was enough for me.

The islands loomed in the distance, a peppering of land far out to sea.

"Is that your home?" she asked, but I couldn't read anything from her neutral tone.

Tension tightened around my spine. I was doing my best to make sure everyone was provided for, but it was never enough.

"The salty air must smell wonderful all the time," she said.

"It's briny."

"It's new to me. The water's gorgeous. Can you see it from your home?"

"*Our* home," I said, though I didn't snap. It would

take time for her to accept this as her new home; that was to be expected.

"All right. *Our* home."

"I live in a house overlooking the sea. It's been in my family for a few generations."

"Do you sit outside in the morning and grin at the view?"

I hadn't in so long, I couldn't remember. "I've got a stone deck where you can sit. I have chairs there."

"Will you join me?"

"Yes."

She relaxed against me as Zarran flew lower. "Where does your vox live?"

"Once we dismount, he'll fly to his nest on one of the uninhabited islands."

"I know nothing about voxes."

"I'll take you to the hatching grounds sometime, though they're far from here. It's very dry there and mostly made up of sand, though there are pools with islands that will amaze you."

She nodded and studied the land we flew over. "How many live on our island?"

I grinned at her use of *our*. "Thirty, the largest group of them clustered in the village center. Our house is within walking distance."

"A small group, then. You must know each of them well."

"I know them as best I can. They . . . sometimes hold themselves away from me, as they did with my father. Such is the way of the caedos and his people."

"As your mate, will they expect me to do the same?"

"I don't know."

"How was it with your mother?"

"She adored everyone." My smile rose, though it was tinged with sadness. "And they adored her."

"How about you?"

"I'm the person I always was."

She said nothing as we passed over small dwellings.

A few of my people worked outside in their gardens. One lifted his arm to wave.

"We keep the gardens small. Unless it rains, we have no water. And if it doesn't rain, the crops die." *We* died. Or moved to the city.

"Do you have wells?"

"The ground's too rocky to dig them."

"And the sea? The islands project up from an enormous body of water."

"It's salty. It kills the plants."

"I see."

"We can't drink it either," I added. "Though it's full of fish, so we never go hungry." Not for meat, that is.

We approached my home that faced the vast ocean opposite the side facing the city, and Zarran swooped lower.

"I'm excited to see where you—we'll—live."

Would her excitement hold? I shouldn't feel bad about the island where I grew up. "We live simply."

"I'm fine with that. Zur and I shared a small . . . I guess you'd call it a shack when compared to the beautiful buildings in the city. Two tiny bedrooms so small you can barely walk around the sleeping surface. One open area where we cooked and sat in the evening. I guess someone else will claim it now. I hope they give Zur a good burial."

Her arm lifted toward the open world beyond the island where the deep purple sea gleamed in the sunlight, broken only with whitecaps. "What's in that direction? More islands?"

"This island chain is the last as far as I know. None of my people have flown far enough in that direction to find out what must be out there."

"It must end eventually. There's land behind us."

"Maybe the sea doesn't end until it reaches the other end of the land behind us."

"Like your people, few humans have traveled far. It's too dangerous with the shaydes and who knows what else, and why bother? Everything we need can be found inside the village or in the surrounding area."

Except me. I hoped she'd someday see that, feel that. I couldn't be found within her village.

Why had my clan chosen this remote, harsh place to live? If only I could offer her something better. We could move to the city, but I'd waste away there. My heart and feet were planted deeply in the island, and I couldn't imagine uprooting them.

But it was all we could do to grow the food we needed. Water was more precious than coin. Yes, we could buy food in the city and bring it to the island, but there was a reason our population dropped instead of expanding. We lacked women, but our males still chose to leave. They fled to the city to find jobs, at first stating they'd be back. Later stating they'd return next year or the one after that.

Few felt a strong bond to the island.

The old remained, plus a few hardened warriors.

And me.

Zarran landed on a broad stretch of tall grass that swished and swooped in the salty breeze. The vast ocean stretched beyond the island for as far as I could see, and I knew I'd never tire of gazing at its beauty.

Trees grew on the island, but they were stubby and scruffy, probably due to the sandy soil and less rainfall. Nevertheless, the island would produce what could best survive in this environment. Like the orcs who lived here.

And now me.

"Is it safe to wander around?" I asked as Odik removed our belongings from the spike on Zarran's neck and swung them over his shoulder. "Not now, but in general."

"We always need to be concerned about dresalod attacks, though we'll hear them coming."

"You mentioned they shriek." Not an exciting prospect.

"Not only that, but the cliffs are made up of shale. When the dresalods crawl across the surface, small pieces break off and rattle as they fall. We hear that and know they're climbing."

"What about during a storm? It would be hard to hear them then."

"They don't leave the sea during a storm. They hide deep below the surface."

"At least you don't have to worry about them during that time." I frowned as I looked around, noting rocks bigger than my head in piles near the edge of the cliff. "Don't you run out of boulders?"

"We collect them and bring them back to the surface. It's hard work, but this simple system keeps us safe. As I said, the dresalods don't attack often, every six months or so. They're more interested in the city for some reason."

More people to eat? I shuddered at the thought.

"They're ruthless," he said. "Relentless. And they'll rip apart anyone in their path. They eat us, so I want you to always carry a weapon on you."

I bit down on my lower lip, nodding. "I'm not very good with weapons."

"That's why I'm here. But truly, if you see or hear one, find me. Run as fast as you can. Get away from it. I'll do all I can to shield you."

I loved that he was determined to protect me, but I couldn't hover beside him all the time.

"I'll take you into the city soon to get you more clothing," he said.

"Just material if that's available. I worked as a seam-stress and my embroidery is exquisite, if I do say so myself," I said proudly. "Though I don't imagine there will be much call for that here."

"There are still females living on the island, though less in number than males. If they can't bond with a mate here, they leave to find one. We encourage them to bring their new mate back, of course."

"I can make clothing for you too," I said. "I only need material and thread. A few other things."

"Then I'll take you to the city for those."

"Thank you."

As Zarran leaped up and flew away, Odik took my hand and led me toward the weathered building over-looking the sea.

"It's cute," I said, studying the sturdy wooden frame. "Bigger than I expected."

"There are only five rooms, though if need be, I'll enlarge it."

My pulse picked up with anticipation. What would it be like to live in a place not controlled by others? No rent as far as I knew, and no one poised to tell me I'd have to move soon. "Five is more than I had in the village."

"Perhaps one day, the fates will gift us with orclings. We'll need room for them."

"I've never considered having children." Why would I? No one would have me. "I'd love a baby, though." My heart melted at the thought of holding a child, raising it to be strong and confident. Loving it.

And when I pictured that child, it had Odik's strong

jawline and green skin.

I was getting ahead of myself. We had a ways to go before anything like that might happen, but I was going to relax and savor each moment that might bring us in that direction.

He led me along an overgrown walkway lined with wildflowers, and I couldn't stop grinning.

Looking down at me, he frowned. "It looks horrible. I should've done something with it."

"I don't mind weeding." Already, my mind was coming up with ideas. I'd noticed sand along the shore at the base of the cliff as we passed over it. If I could bring some up here, I could reset the stones in the walk. It would be easy to pull the grass and leave the flowers behind. "It's going to look pretty when I'm done with it."

He grunted, his frown remaining.

Swinging open the door, he gestured for me to enter ahead of him. "As I said, it's not much."

It was a home. *My* home.

I stopped inside the entry area and my grin didn't falter when I took in the small kitchen on the right with a window overlooking the sea. On the left, a living area held chairs that were too large for me but looked soft, and a small hallway stretched beyond. A double set of windows in the living area looked out at the cute meadow where Zarran had landed.

"My mother insisted on a washroom, so you'll find that down the hall, as well as three bedrooms. There's a pump there as well as in the kitchen, but the water comes from the sea, so it's as salty as everything else."

"*Three* bedrooms?"

"My mother hoped for many orclings. Unfortunately, they only had me."

"I'm sorry. You must miss her."

"More than anything."

He was so sad; I didn't need to push myself to hug him. His arms splayed out as if he was surprised by the gesture, but I had a lot of affection to give. When I hugged him, Zur would pat my shoulder. He told me once he wasn't much of a hugger, but he'd never received one until me. Because I sensed he was uncomfortable, I gave hugs sparingly. Due to the villagers scorning me, I'd starved emotionally. I could only hope Odik was more like me.

His arms went around me, and I pressed myself against him harder. So far, so good.

Curling forward, he kissed the top of my head. "You're spoiling me."

"With affection?" I grinned at him. "You're spoiling me with this lovely home."

"It's not lovely," he protested. "Truly. You haven't seen its flaws yet, but you will."

I stepped away from him and limped into the kitchen, where I twirled around, my arms lifting. "It's pretty and perfect and it's going to look even better." I'd put wildflowers in a jar on the wooden table. And make curtains for the windows. Pillows for the sofa, and I could make patch quilts with the scraps for all the beds.

Odik just stared at me, his jaw slightly unhinged.

He must've thought I was out of my mind, but truly, I was just happy.

"Show me the bedrooms," I said eagerly.

I followed him down the hall, poking my head into the washroom and gushing when I saw the tub.

"Salt water," he said again. "Remember. And it's cold except in summer."

I wasn't sure how it was pumped to this level, but I was going to find out.

"I can still take a bath inside my very own washroom," I cried. "I can heat the salt water and it'll feel wonderful. No bugs and no ice to break on the surface like the river back at the village."

His brow ridge lifted, and he moved past the small room and down the hall, pointing to the two smaller bedrooms and the big one taking up the end.

A huge bed had been placed in the center of the last, and it was covered in thick blankets. Two windows, one on each side, looked toward the sea and the meadow. And a tall bureau stood along one wall with enough drawers for both of us.

"My room." He coughed. "Yours now too."

My breath caught. "You expect me to sleep with you."

"You're my mate."

"Very well."

His frown deepened. "I told you I won't do anything you don't want me to do. Not until you're ready."

Already, my body hummed at the idea of lying beside him. Of touching him.

How long could I hold myself back?

CHAPTER 17

ODIK

Someone knocked on the door, and Eleri followed me back to the entryway.

"You're here. Finally," Trilden said, bustling inside.

"Yes, finally," Drabass said, entering behind Trilden.

Trilden, I was happy to see. Drabass could wait outside. However, I was caedos of all those living on the island and that included him.

Trilden gave Eleri a steady look before nodding my way. "I see you found success."

Drabass grunted, his lips curling up slightly in a sneer.

"This is Eleri, my mate," I said, my chest expanding with pride. The hunt had been a success—for me. Perhaps the clan fates would choose Trilden for the next hunt? Drabass could remain single for all I cared. Or move to the city. Why did only the most needed males move away?

"Welcome." Trilden bowed to Eleri. "We have so few females here on the island. And a mate for the caedos! We should arrange for a clan gathering to introduce you, don't you think, Drabass?" He elbowed Drabass. Like me and Trilden, they'd been friends since they were little. Drabass, however, had never treated me as a friend. It didn't help that I defeated his father for the role of caedos. Drabass must've seen the chance to inherit rule from his father.

Frankly, ruling was a duty, not a gift, though I doubted Drabass would ever see it that way. To him, the position represented power, and he wasn't wrong in that. But how the power was used was the difference. Drabass might wield it like a sword to force others to behave the way he wanted, while I would persuade and lead with an example I wished others to follow.

"A celebration sounds like an excellent idea." I braced Trilden's shoulder. "You said *finally*? Is everything going smoothly here?" As my second, Trilden often stepped in to cover for me when I couldn't be on the island to handle issues.

His smile faded, and he sighed. "Three more have left."

My heart went stone cold. "Who this time?"

"Breard, Zainest, and Zainest's son, Timend."

"They moved to the city?" That left only twenty-seven of us on the island. At this rate, I'd be caedos of only me, Eleri, and Trilden before the year ended.

"They took jobs there."

Then they weren't coming back soon unless I could

find a way to entice them, and there was no hope for that. The island lifestyle only worked if there was enough food to sustain us. To grow food, we needed water.

Sometimes, I felt like giving up, but each time my will wavered, I shored up my spine and led my people as my ancestors had done before me. "Perhaps they'll reconsider."

Trilden shrugged. "I'd love it if they did."

But we both knew they wouldn't.

Drabass nodded, though his gaze remained fixed on Eleri, not me. His expression remained neutral, but I still didn't like him staring at her.

"Other than that, I've been helping the rest prepare for the incoming storm," Trilden said.

What storm?

I strode to the window facing the vast open sea and growled.

"What is it?" Eleri asked, joining me.

"A tempest is coming."

She frowned and looked out the window. "A storm? It looks calm out there, though I don't know how to gauge a vast body of water like this one. When a storm approaches the village, we see dark clouds to the west, and the wind picks up, swirling around us. Zur said you could always tell a storm was coming when the leaves on the trees flipped over, revealing their paler undersides."

"Look there." I pointed to the ominous strip of darkness burgeoning along the horizon. "A day, maybe two at best before it hits."

"Since you were still away, I made sure everyone was

notified," Trilden said. "We've begun covering the windows in the community gathering area, and I've sent males to those living in the more isolated areas to make sure they're aware and lend any assistance they might need."

"Thank you." I was grateful to have Trilden as a second. Would Drabass have stepped into my place and started the preparations? I doubted it.

Eleri's wide eyes met mine. "I'm not sure what to expect from a storm at sea." A shiver tracked through her, and she wrapped her arms around her waist, holding herself.

I gave her a level look that I hoped would give her some reassurance. "We'll be ready when it arrives, but I need to leave you now and work with Trilden and Drabass to get ready."

"I'm sorry for taking your mate from you so soon," Trilden told her. "I realize you've just arrived."

"I'm fine alone," she said, keeping her tone light. Her eyes spoke volumes, however. She was nervous, perhaps because of the storm. She knew nothing about what it was like to live on an island or among an orc clan.

"Let me make sure she's settled," I told them. "I'll join you two at the community center."

Trilden gave me a sharp nod, then bowed to Eleri again before leaving.

Drabass's gaze lingered on her before he sauntered out of our home.

"I'll finish showing you around." I opened the cold box that thankfully still held food. Long ago, orcs discovered a way to pipe the coolness from deep below the surface and use it to keep a box made out of special material cold. Food could then be stored in the box to be eaten over a few days. "After I make sure everyone's prepared to weather the storm, I need to fish. We'll store enough food to hold us through the tempest."

"Do you have a boat?"

"I fish from the smooth boulders on the edge of the sea." I braced her forearms and looked down at her. "I'll take you with me if you'd like." My grin slipped out. Despite my concern about the storm, I was still grateful she was with me. I looked forward to getting to know her better.

And taking her to my bed.

But that would have to wait. Until we were ready to weather anything the sea might throw our way, I couldn't relax within my home with Eleri.

"What can I do to help get ready?" she asked, nodding sharply. The fear that had flitted through her eyes was gone, replaced with resolve. This female could be strong when it mattered most.

"I'll cover the windows when I return. I've done that so many times, it's easier to do it than tell you how to do it for me. Otherwise, I scour the area and put anything loose inside the shed nestled close to the patch of trees. I sunk the footers deep, and the shed won't go anywhere, no matter how strong the wind is. If you put loose things inside, they won't fly around and be lost or potentially cause damage."

"What about the voxes?"

"They'll sense the storm coming and prepare in their own way."

"All right. I'll do what I can." She sent me a smile and nudged me away. "Go. Do what you need to do to get things ready for our people. I'll find my way here and walk around outside, collecting anything I can."

"You're amazing. I can't tell you how much I appreciate your help and your . . ."

"The fact that I'm not a wreck?" She laughed. "Inside, I am, but I don't want to hold you back. Go help everyone and come back to me."

"Oh, I will. You can count on that."

I kissed her quickly, wishing I could linger longer, then darted through the door.

It was only when I'd caught up to Trilden and Drabass that I realized that was our first kiss.

I'd barely had time to savor it.

CHAPTER 18

ELERI

After eating something quickly, I went outside, first walking around the perimeter of the house. I stood for a brief time at the wooden fence spanning the top of the cliff overlooking the sea that stretched on forever, noting how smooth the cliff face was and where the boulders were in case I needed to grab and drop one.

If I couldn't lift one, I'd roll it over the side.

The smudge of darkness on the horizon hadn't expanded, but they'd said the storm wouldn't arrive for a day or two.

Did we have time to get ready?

I'd weathered storms in the village but back then, Zur was with me, and our neighbors would help if we had great need. Help Zur, that is. I was less sure they'd ever help me.

That didn't appear to be the case here, at least with Trilden. Drabass? I wasn't sure about him. He was friendly and appeared to be Odik's friend, but I hadn't liked how he'd looked at me.

What would it be like to live among people who accepted and welcomed me? I hoped I'd find out. Here, I felt like I had a chance.

The cliff plunged down below me, landing at broad smooth rocks stretching away from the sandy shore. Odik's fishing spot, most likely. Waves glided up to the rocks and when they hit, sprayed water into the air. So pretty. I could only imagine how treacherous it might be down there when the storm arrived.

"Get to work," I told myself. "No more taking in the gorgeous view."

I limped toward the house, planning to walk in widening circles around it.

I found a rake, a few containers covered with overgrown grass, and a pile of boards near the spindly cluster of trees. I put the containers and rake in the shed, securing the bar on the outside, but left the boards where they were for now. They appeared to have been there a while and were grayed from the weather. They must've been through many storms. I'd ask Odik about them when he returned.

After walking back and forth across the meadow and not finding anything else, I decided to take the path I'd seen in the woods. I wouldn't walk far, though it was good for my leg to get the exercise. Curiosity drove me to explore my new world.

The path meandered through the woods, exiting at another meadow. I could see what Odik had alluded to in the large garden area. Scruffy crops in neat rows struggled to survive, the sun baking them. I picked those that were mature to bring into the house and mulched around as many of the plants as I could with leaves gathered from beneath the trees. The wind would sweep them away, but until the storm arrived, the mulch would help preserve the moisture. Dew must form here just like it did in the village gardens, and that would quench the plants a little.

At least the storm should bring rain. I'd make sure we had barrels and containers set up to collect it, though I was sure Odik did that already. Where else would we get drinking water?

I also found a series of open stone tubs overgrown with weeds along the edge of the meadow, but I couldn't imagine what they might be used for. Perhaps to collect the rain.

After clearing them of weeds, I returned to the house with my skirt loaded with vegetables from the garden. Were there any fruit trees that needed picking? Returning outside, I walked around, finding a small tree with orange fruit. But I wasn't sure if they were edible or ripe. I'd wait to ask Odik.

Since he'd be hungry when he returned, I prepared him a simple meal and put the plate in the cool box.

Night had fallen before Odik arrived, and he was clearly exhausted.

After washing his hands beneath the saltwater pump at the sink, he dropped into a chair and sighed. I placed his meal on the table where he could reach it.

"Thank you," he said, taking a big bite of the bread with meat and cheese I'd made him. "This is good."

I nodded, smiling.

"Is everyone ready?" I sat across from him, worrying the placemat in front of me.

"I believe so. I'll check again tomorrow."

"I'll come with you if you'd like." I wanted to meet everyone.

"That would be wonderful." He reached across the table and took my hand, squeezing it. "I owe you an apology."

"For what?"

"Our first kiss was so quick; I doubt you felt it."

Heat rose into my cheeks. "We've passed the kissing stage, haven't we?"

"You don't like kissing?"

I'd enjoyed his kiss even if it had been brief. "Perhaps we need to do it a few more times before I decide."

He grinned. "I'll be glad to accommodate you, mate."

My smile joined with his, and once again, I was grateful I'd taken the other woman's place in the hunt.

No one believed something good could come from the hunt, but they were wrong. The fates had given me the best life had to offer and it was Odik. Already, I was falling for this solemn, kind male, and I could easily love him. He was like the warmth of a snuggly blanket.

And the heat I'd find beneath it.

I gestured to my haul from the garden, and he nodded, his gaze full of pride when he looked back at me.

I loved feeling needed.

"You've been busy," he said, speaking around another bite. "I appreciate the help."

Being a good mate to him mattered a lot to me. He appeared to carry all the clan's burdens, and I wanted him to know he could share them with me. Life here wouldn't be easy, that was clear already, but if we shared the work, surely we could find joy in what we did because we'd be together.

I told him what I'd done in the garden and mentioned the pile of wood.

"It can stay where it is. I'll make sure the ties I fixed to the ground a year or so ago are secure, but we don't need to carry any of it into the shed."

"Look around in the morning to make sure I didn't miss anything."

He nodded.

"I'm going fishing and then for a swim," he announced after he'd swallowed his last bite. Rising, he took his plate to the sink and carefully washed it.

"Fishing in the dark?" Let alone swimming. I'd splashed along the shore of the river but only during daylight hours.

"The fish come close to shore at night to feed. With a hook and some bait, I can bring in a good catch." Turning, he leaned against the counter. "We'll clean them and store them in the cool box, so we have plenty to eat during the storm. I'll try to catch enough for those who can't fish."

"I've cleaned many fish," I said. "Zur was a good hunter and fisherman. He sold most of it, and we used that income, plus mine from my work as a seamstress, to buy or barter for everything else we needed. As I said, I made all our clothing.”

“There’s a need for a seamstress here. We purchase our clothing in the city.”

“Maybe once things are settled, I can open a small shop.” That would benefit us both and the community.

“Or you could set up a shop in the city.”

“And travel there each day?” I wondered how that would work.

“Zarran could take us. Or . . .” He looked down at his boots. “We could stay there most of the time.”

Was he shoving me out the door already? No, he couldn’t be. He seemed to be happy having me here with him. Perhaps he meant we’d remain in the city together.

“Are you thinking of leaving the island?” I asked carefully.

“I love it here. It’s been my clan’s home for many generations, longer than anyone can remember, but each time a few leave, then a few more, it makes it harder for the rest of us to survive.” When he lifted his gaze, a profound sadness filled his eyes.

My chest ached in sympathy. “What would you do if we lived in the city?”

“I could sign with the army. My friend Jaus is the commander of the entire fleet.”

“Army.” I pondered what that could mean. “I assume they defend the city.”

“Yes,” he said grimly. “From both shaydes and the dresalods.”

And I could lose him.

I shouldn't cling. Everyone had to fight off attacks or none would survive. Still, I couldn't imagine losing him.

"We can talk about that later." He nudged his head toward the hall. "Let me gather some things together, and we can take the stairs to the bottom of the cliff."

I hadn't seen any stairs, but I'd spent most of my time scanning the meadows and area around the house for things to pack away.

"Would you like your first swimming lesson tonight?" he asked.

"In the dark?"

"You'll be perfectly safe."

I should be frightened of the idea of fish nibbling on my toes, right? But if Odik was with me, I wasn't. "All right."

He started toward the bedroom but turned back to look my way. "By the way. I always swim naked."

I threw the comment out there mostly to see how she'd react. She'd been sweetly responsive to my touch so far, but I wasn't sure how far I wanted—or dared—to push this. We were growing closer. I was half in love with her already.

I wanted more, though I would never coerce her into doing anything she wasn't as excited about as me.

"I think," she said, rising from her chair. "That I'll learn to swim while naked."

There was my brave mate. My heartrate doubled in a flash, and I whistled merrily as I strode to the washroom and collected drying cloths. My fishing equipment was inside the shed, and we could grab it on our way.

Heat charged through my veins, and my cock rose to the occasion. Good thing I still wore a loose loincloth and not pants, or I'd tent them.

I returned to the kitchen to find her waiting with a look I couldn't interpret on her face. Not trepidation.

This woman had more courage than an attacking dresalod legion.

Anticipation?

Yes, that was it.

We left the house, stopping at the shed to collect my fishing supplies and the container I'd use to bring my catch back to the house. We'd clean it on the shore and leave the entrails and scales in the water. After, I led her toward the stairs a prior generation had carved into the face of the stony cliff ages ago.

"Are you excited about swimming or . . .?" I let the rest of the question hang so she could take it in any direction she pleased.

"Both."

Ha. I loved how she tossed my dare right back at me.

Perhaps I wouldn't analyze this. I'd let it play out as it was supposed to.

"Ah, I didn't see these here earlier," she said as we started down the stairs. She held the drying cloths and even the height didn't seem to scare her, though there was a rail between us and the steep drop-off.

"They let out on the sandy shore. The last twenty feet are made of wood and can be pulled up if the dresalods attack."

"Wise."

I nodded. "Thankfully, dresalods can't jump very high. I fish off the big rocks you might've seen earlier if you looked over the cliff."

"I did see them. It's beautiful here, even at night." She paused on the stairs and tipped her head back, taking in the stars and the full moon overhead. Pointing toward the sea, her smile grew. "Look how the light glistens on the water. A storm may be brewing, but for now, I see only beauty."

"The sea is a dangerous female, my father always said."

"Such a huge body of water. So much power."

"If you treat her right, she'll reward you, my father also said."

"He sounds wise."

"He was. Stern, but kind enough. He adored my mother. I don't believe he could've gone on without her."

"Did he know she'd died?"

"He didn't." We started walking down the stairs again. "They likely died at about the same time. He'd gone to the city for the day and joined the dresalods battle. He was killed not long after they attacked, snatched from his vox. I was here, handling affairs my father left in my care. My mother had gone down to the rocks to fish. The dresalods attacked everywhere at once and when she didn't return, I sought her. There was blood . . ." It was everywhere, and nothing was left of her.

I hated voicing even a bit of what I saw when I went looking for my mother.

Eleri's hand landed on my shoulder, and she squeezed. "I'm sorry. She'd be grateful you survived."

"I know she would." Her loss still burned through my belly. For a long time, I wondered if me being with her could've increased her odds of survival. I could've protected her, gotten her to safety. But I wasn't, and I'd learned to accept that.

"Fishing or swimming first?" she asked as we left the staircase.

"We'll go fishing, clean the fish, and put the catch in the container on the stairs to bring up after. Then we'll go swimming—though not where we dump the guts. I know the perfect place to take you where the sea isn't rough, and you'll feel completely secure."

"Dresalods?"

"It's always a risk, but we'll remain close to the stairs."

"All right."

With moonlight guiding us, we walked across the pebbled shore and up onto the broad rocks that had been here since the dawn of time. I lowered my supplies onto a rock close to where the water lapped against the lower stones and watched the water for a long time. No bubbles or ripples to show dresalods were rising to the surface. It should be safe enough for a bit, though I'd keep watching.

"Can I fish too?" Eleri asked.

"I brought two poles just in case. I'll bait them, and we can cast them out. Whoever catches the most fish owes the other something."

She scrunched up her face. "That sounds rather broad."

"What would you like me to give you if you catch the most fish?" I baited one of the hooks and handed her the pole while she tapped her chin, thinking about it.

She grinned mischievously and leaned close, her palm resting on my chest. "Oh, I think I have an idea, my dear orc," she whispered, her voice filled with playful suggestion.

I raised an eyebrow, my curiosity piqued.

"Do tell," I said, a smirk tugging at the corners of my lips.

She bit down on her bottom lip, her eyes gleaming. I'd never seen anyone as prettier than Eleri in the moonlight. "If I catch the most fish, you'll have to sing to me."

I chuckled, enjoying how she challenged me. "What if I can't sing well?"

She shrugged. "It'll still be you serenading me. That's enough."

"Very well." What should I ask for if I won the game? "If I catch the most fish, you'll have to dance with me."

"What if I can't dance?" she quipped.

"I don't mind leading."

"I'm surprised."

"That an orc can dance? My mother taught me when I was little, though I'll be honest and tell you that I haven't danced since." There was no one else I'd ever wanted to dance with but my mom.

And now Eleri.

"Tell you what," I said. "If I win, I'll dance with you and sing to provide the music."

"So I get to hear you sing no matter who wins." She smiled. "I like that. It's a deal."

After casting our lines into the calm sea, we settled on the end of the largest and highest rock, letting our legs dangle. Moonlight shimmered on the gentle waves.

"It's hard to believe a storm will ravage this area soon," Eleri said, leaning against my side. "It's calm and peaceful."

"That's how it always is. The world lulls you, making you believe the darkness on the horizon is just a tease. Then the storm hits."

As we waited for the fish to nibble, I sucked in the salty air mixed with the sweet fragrance of the beach flowers blooming nearby. The sound of distant seabirds echoed through the quiet night, adding to the peaceful ambiance.

"Trilden said three of your clan have moved to the city," she said.

"They're not the first, as you probably guessed. The population is slowly diminishing on the island, not growing as I'd like. If most of our females hadn't been killed, perhaps things would be different."

"Things always look better when the laughter of children rings out in the air. I won't be the first mate from the village. Maybe Trilden and some of the other males will bond with women over the next few years. They'd bring their mates here, and the population would slowly replenish."

"I live for that day."

"Why haven't *you* left? I know you're the leader of your clan, but you could move everyone to the city if their lives will be better there."

"*Will* their lives be better?" I thought about it for a

moment. "Look around you. What could be more wonderful than sitting here fishing with the moonlight shining down on us?"

"You could sit in the moonlight and fish on the shore outside the city."

"But I wouldn't feel free." How could I explain what was only a feeling? "The sounds of the city would encroach. People talking, laughing, moving about."

"All good things."

"Here, there's nothing but us and the sea."

"And the storm that will ravage this small island soon."

"We'll rebuild if we have to. We'll go on."

"I love it here already," she said. "There's a serenity, a feeling of peace here that I never experienced in the village. There, it was crowded with small homes built almost on top of each other. Even within our small building, it felt like the world was trying to crowd inside with us."

Maybe she *did* see.

"There are jobs in the city," she said.

"I can't see myself going to work in the morning, laboring all day, only to repeat the same thing again the next day. Doing so until my body is worn out and too tired to savor something as simple as fishing or . . ." I sent her a smile. "Or sitting here with you on the rocks, Eleri." I continued before she could speak. "I'm busy enough with my caedos duties, but even more, I feel as if I'm a caretaker of these islands and this quieter way of life. I do as my father did before me and his mother before him. Whatever my people need, I find a way to provide."

Except they kept leaving, and with each one, it felt as if they took a chunk of my heart along with them.

"We need to find a way to get people to move to the island, then," she said fiercely. "It's beautiful here even if danger looms on the horizon. As you said, you can rebuild if you need to. It can't be much different in the city. The storm will pass over us and barrel toward them."

I didn't point out that they had the city wall as protection from the worst the rising sea could hurtle their way, that their shiny silver homes shed the rain and withstood the wind with ease.

Instead, I sat on the stone feeling completely humbled because I'd found someone who understood.

My clan pendant may have chosen this woman to stand beside me for the rest of my days, but she wanted to be here with me. There was a difference, and I'd do all I could to keep her from ever feeling any other way.

She was the shelter my heart needed.

We talked about island life, our voices blending harmoniously with the lapping of the water against the rocks. My heart soared, knowing that this male, with his quick wit and infectious laughter, was slowly weaving his way into the depths of my heart. I kept stealing glances at him, captivated by the way the moonlight lit up his features.

Minutes ticked on as we sat side by side.

"I'm beginning to think the fish have decided to spend the night preparing their homes for the coming tempest," I said. "They're not biting."

"They're here. We just have to woo them. Like *you*, mate. I'm wooing you."

He was right. It was nice sitting here with him, talking with him. He opened his heart to me, and I treasured that he felt comfortable doing so with me.

Something tugged on my line, and I gasped, scrambling up to stand on the rock.

I carefully rolled my line in, but when the hook emerged from the sea, it was empty.

"Something stole my bait," I said, scowling at the water.

"I'll add more." Odik soon had me back in business again, my line drifting deeper into the gorgeous sea.

Finally, my patience paid off.

My line skimmed out to sea as if the fish hoped to catch the storm, but I held tight, slowly bringing it in.

"You've got it," Odik cried, standing behind me with his hands resting on my arms, ready to help me haul in my catch if I had need.

I wiggled in anticipation.

When I tugged the last of the line from the water, I held up a fish about the length of my arm. It was such a heavy thing that it was all I could do to hold it aloft long enough to brag.

"Looks like I'm winning," I teased, leaning back in his arms triumphantly.

He groaned. "You might be ahead for now, but the night is young, little mate."

As if the sea heard his challenge, a sudden surge of activity filled the water beneath us, a school of fish swarming around his line.

After removing the hook from my fish, I placed it in the container, then quickly rebaited my line, tossing it into the water while the fish still swarmed beneath us.

"Go, bait, go," I cried. "Do your thing and give me another fish!"

Time seemed to stand still as we hauled in one fish

after another. Our laughter skipped across the water, mixing with the gentle swirl of the water on the rocks below. While the moon bathed everything in its ethereal glow, it was his presence that truly illuminated my world.

I was falling in love with him, and I didn't want to hold myself back. He was kind and gentle, and he had an old soul, one I wanted to hold in my hands and keep safe. I hated that the world was determined to hurt him, and I wanted to create a place for him where he could feel secure.

That would be with me.

As the night progressed, we laughed and shared bits from our lives. With catch after catch, the scales kept tipping in his favor.

"How many fish do we want to catch?" I asked as I pulled in my fifth. Or was it my sixth? "We're going to be eating fish for the rest of our lives."

"We'll share. Some who live on the island can't get around as well as they used to. I provide for them and do all I can to make their lives easy."

He kept giving to everyone around him.

I wanted to give to him.

"As for how many, I think we've got enough." He glanced back at the overflowing container. "We still need to clean them, but I can do that while you sit and savor what's probably your victory."

"I think we might be even, though it's hard to tell. We didn't identify who caught what."

He smiled down at me. "A draw then?"

"I think so, though I've still won, because you're going to sing!" My laughter pealed out.

His low chuckle joined in. "My mother always said I have an amazing voice."

"I can't wait to hear it."

"Could I persuade you to hold off on collecting your victory prize until tomorrow night?"

"Why not now? You can sing me to sleep or share your tune while we clean the fish."

"I want to set up a nice evening for you tomorrow and singing will be part of it."

"The storm may be here by then."

"We can do this inside. I know a special place."

I couldn't wait. Each moment with Odik felt better than the last, and I was beginning to believe this was the future I could look forward to.

He handed me our poles and lifted the container, his muscles bulging from the load. I doubted I could lift it, but he strode along the rock with ease, hopping down onto the rocky shore.

We cleaned the fish, never a fun task. After rinsing out the container, we placed our catch inside, and he shut the lid.

"Let's take this up to the house and store the fish in the cool box. I've got a second inside the shed we can use if we need to." He smiled down at me. "And then, my pretty mate, I believe it's time for your swimming lesson."

CHAPTER 21

ODIK

We put the fish in the cool box, and I was grateful to see such a large catch. This would be enough to carry not just us through the storm but all the others I supported. During the day, I'd made sure their homes were secure, covering their windows and tying down or bringing anything the tempest might steal inside. It was important to check up on them frequently, and a storm was as good an excuse as any.

After washing our hands at the sink, I turned and leaned against the counter.

"We left the drying cloths down on the rocks," Eleri said, her face open and cheerful in the light of the whisp lanterns. I crossed the room and blew on each to keep them glowing.

"We'll pick them up on our way to where we'll swim."

A smile teased across her lips. "Where *will* we swim?

The sea was calm beyond the rocks, but when I looked over the cliffs, I could see spray lifting in some areas. Don't we have to worry about dresalods or being pushed against the boulders?"

"I'm going to show you where it's safe, mate." Taking her hand, I led her back outside and down the stairs again. But instead of going left and to the boulders, I took her along the shore to the right, all the way to the point and around it.

"It's so pretty," she said, looking from the sea to me.

"Are you saying I'm pretty?" I teased.

"Very much." Her laughter spilled out, and I adored how content she seemed just being with me. I could envision a long, happy life with her. It might not be easy, but we'd face each challenge together.

"I think you're the pretty one, not me."

"You're sweet, Odik. I was frightened about what I'd face when I left the fortress, but what I've found with you is much more than I could've ever have imagined."

"I don't imagine you thought you'd find anything good with the orcs."

"We're mistaken. I'll tell them if I ever return." A shadow slipped across her face, stealing her joy. "Of course, I can never return. They think I murdered Zur. They'll arrest me."

"If there was a way to clear your name, I would."

"Thank you." She shrugged. "I hate that the few people I could call friends would believe I could do something horrible like that. They knew I loved him."

Her chin lifted. "You know what? I bet they don't believe I did it, and I hope they speak up and say so."

I hoped they did too. We could return to the village, and she could tell them what happened from the safety of the forest, but would it make a difference? If they didn't believe her, they'd try to capture her. I'd never put my mate in danger.

Because I loved her.

The feeling had slipped so easily into my heart, as if that organ knew a piece was missing and waited only for her to slip it into place. Some might say it was fast and sudden, but that was the way with fated mates.

"Where are you taking me?" she said with a low laugh.

I was glad she could shrug off her sadness and focus on now.

"Not far." I led her up a small hill and down the other side, approaching a series of flat rocks like the ones we'd fished from.

"Will we jump off these?" She released a shiver. "I'm not sure if I'm ready to plunge into the sea when it's over my head."

"We'll swim where it's shallow and safe."

"In this huge body of water? We caught some good-sized fish, and that tells me that the things that eat them are bigger than the ones we reeled in."

"There are enormous fish in the sea. I've seen them in the spring. They migrate, and as they pass in huge schools, they leap from the water and splash back down among their friends. Their skin is smooth, not scaled.

The tops of their bodies are dark purple and the underside paler."

"I can't wait to see them, but honestly, I don't want to swim with them."

"You won't."

We crossed a series of huge flat rocks and stopped in the middle.

"A pool," she exclaimed. "It's in the middle of the rocks, though I can see that water splashes up across the front of the boulders and keeps it filled." Her gaze followed the water-filled channel all the way to the cliffs, and she pointed. "Is that a cave?"

"It's shallow." I'd explored every part of this island when I was young. "Sadly, there's no excitement in that direction." I reached for the tie to my loincloth. "Ready for your first swimming lesson?"

"I suspect you have more than swimming in mind, *mate*."

"Are you all right with that?" She'd given me the idea she was falling for me just like I was for her, but perhaps she wasn't ready to take this further.

"I am." She lifted her top over her head and tossed it aside, revealing her glorious breasts.

As I unwound the leather and dropped it on the rocks, she shimmied out of her skirt and laid it carefully next to her folded top.

Her shoes joined the rest of her clothing, and she straightened, her chin lifted slightly. "My leg's a mess. Please don't look at it."

"I saw it when I massaged it, remember?"

"It was dark then."

"It's dark now." I dropped to my knees in front of her, though this put us at eye level. "I see scars, but they're badges of courage. They show me you're a fighter, that you don't give up, that no matter what happens to you, you keep trying." I met her gaze, and I hoped she could see the honesty in mine. "I cherish each part of you, including your scars."

"You're going to make me cry." Her lips trembled. "I don't hate my scars, per se. They're so much a part of me now that other than my limp and a wish that my leg would work better than it does, I accept myself as I am. How can I do anything else? It's not as if I can change this."

"You're beautiful," I said in awe. "I still can't believe you're even willing to look at me."

As I rose to my feet, she stepped right up to me, our skin brushing. "You're perfect. Strong, kind, and gorgeous."

"Males aren't gorgeous," I said with a smile. "We're handsome or perhaps striking. Nothing as glorious as you."

"It seems we both admire each other. That's enough, don't you think?"

"It is." I was honored to have this woman as my mate, and I was going to cherish her each and every date the fates granted us.

I couldn't believe we were standing here naked and only talking. She was lovely, all lush curves and creamy skin so different from my green. Her breasts were high and round, and I wanted to suck on her nipples. But despite teasing her about swimming naked, I didn't plan to take this too far. I'd let her guide what we did tonight.

"How will you teach me to swim?" she asked, wrapping her arms around her body.

"Are you uncomfortable being naked with me?"

"I should be, right? But we've done things. Not everything, but we've both seen parts of each other. This . . . just takes it a bit further."

"If you're more comfortable learning to swim with clothing on, we can wear our shirts."

She teased her fingertip across my belly, and my brain shot all the way to the sky. My cock tried to reach it too. Her smile grew as she traced a fingertip along my length.

"Big," she said. "Thick. One of these days, you're going to have to show me what you can do with it."

"Say the word, mate, and I will."

When she looked up at me, her gaze was full of mischief. "Swimming first. We'll talk about other activities after that."

Very well. "As for how I'll teach you," It was all I could do to think—speak—and not stroke every bit of her lovely body. "I'll hold you in the water and show you how to keep your head above the surface, then slowly show you how to move when you challenge the rest of the sea."

"Which I'm not going to do today, right?"

"Maybe we can wait for tomorrow," I teased.

Her head tilted. "During the storm?"

"Maybe we'll wait until a day or two after the storm."

She gripped my forearms. "For whatever reason, I've always been afraid of deep water."

"Maybe that's how you hurt your leg?"

"I don't remember." Her shrug shifted her breasts. Highly distracting. "I was either too young or I've blocked it from my mind."

"Do you want to know?"

"Sometimes, yes. Did I do something stupid or was it an accident or did someone try to harm me? I just don't know." She shrugged. "It doesn't matter any longer."

"Sometimes it's best to just let go of the things you can't change."

"You're right." She stepped back and stared toward the sea stretching on for what seemed like forever. "The clouds are gathering, strengthening. It's going to be a big storm."

I went up behind her and held her, savoring the feel of our bodies touching. I ached to be with her, but it was also nice to just hold her. "When I was young and the mantle of leadership hadn't settled on my shoulders, I used to love storms."

"Do you fear them now?"

"Only what they can do to my people. There's something awesome about a storm. My father used to come down to the rocks where we fished while the tide was out. We'd stand there and challenge the storm's fury with our arms and voices raised."

"I understand. It's doing something, not just letting the storm rush over you while you cower."

"Exactly. When the tide comes in during a storm, the water covers the rocks. This pool as well. It washes against the cave you hoped to explore."

"Are there other caves on the island?"

"If there were," I said, "I would've found them already. I spent much of my childhood exploring every bit of the island. I started doing the same with the uninhabited ones nearby until my father caught me returning one day in his boat and smacked my ass, telling me never to take on the sea alone again."

"How old were you then?"

"Ten."

She laughed and turned in my arms, looking up at me. "I think I would've chided you too if you'd been my son."

I shrugged. "My mother visited the village often. My father was always busy with the clan. I entertained myself."

"I'm sorry. I imagine you were lonely."

"There were other orclings here I played with, but I also enjoyed being by myself." I nudged my chin to the pool. "Enough of that, however. Let's sit on the side first and dangle our feet in the water."

She laughed again when we did so, pointing to where her feet skimmed well above the water. "So much for dangling our feet. I'm coming up short."

I slid off the rock and into the refreshing chill of the pool and faced her with my arms toward her, treading water to hold my position. "Jump in and I'll catch you."

A cute frown took over her face. "How's the temperature?"

"Cool. Wonderful."

"That's a matter of perspective. Some of the wealthier villagers had tubs and would have servants carry hot water to fill it. I can't imagine what it's like to soak in hot water."

"Maybe you'll find out one day." I could heat the sea water. Buy a tub in the city. It would make a wonderful surprise.

She hopped down to join me in the pool, shrieking when her body slid into the water. Bobbing, she clung to my shoulders, and I was reminded all over again that we wore no clothing.

I traced my fingers down her sides, and she shivered, her gaze falling on my mouth.

"I love that this puts us at the right height for kissing, but it is *so* cold!" she said, quaking.

"Kissing, you say? Are you trying to tempt me away from my swim lesson?" Like she needed to make any effort? It was all I could do not to touch her breasts, her luscious ass. To spread her legs and touch her there.

"Why would I want to distract you?" Her eyes gleamed with mischief. "I live on an island surrounded by water. It makes sense for me to learn how to swim, don't you think?"

Because I could never resist her, I kissed her, stroking my tongue across her lips until she gave me full access.

This was our first true kiss, and I was going to savor it.

With a moan, she clutched my shoulders, pressing her body against mine.

I stroked her lips with my tongue, and she let me inside. Our tongues slid together, as did our bodies.

Fuck it. I slid my fingers across her breast and rolled her nipple.

She broke away with a gasp, her eyes dark with desire. "I think you're the one providing a distraction."

"Should I stop?"

"I like it. It would be a lie to say I didn't."

"We came here for your swimming lesson." And it was important that she learn. "What do you say to swimming first, and then I'll show you pleasure?"

"Maybe we should skip the lesson."

Heat roared through me, but the storm was coming. This would be our last time in the water for days.

I was foolish not to take her offer, but I didn't want her to think I brought her down here with the tease of getting naked only to take advantage of the situation. My cock shouted it was well past time I claimed her, but I had principles.

"We'll have a short lesson." Nothing was going to get the image of claiming my mate out of my mind.

She pouted, her bottom lip jutting out in the most tempting way. "You're a tease."

"But you're relaxed in the water now, aren't you?

She huffed. "I am."

"I *am* a tease, but I'm also determined," I said. "We're surrounded by water. While you don't have to swim regularly unless you wish, you should know how to do it.

One day, the lessons I give you could prove vital for your survival."

"You're right." She sent me a rueful look. "What's next?"

"I want you to let go of me and hold onto those rocks on the side. They'll help you feel secure as you learn to swim."

"I could cling to you."

And mess with my fragile self-control? It was all I could do to remember why we were here and not focus on her delectable body.

"Always," I said gruffly. I shook my head and made myself focus. "There may be times you want to swim alone, though please don't do that until we're both confident in your swimming abilities."

"All right." She released her hold on my shoulders, reaching out for the edge of the rocks. Her fingers gripped them tightly, her knuckles turning white with her effort.

"You're doing great." I followed, staying an arm's length away from her, ready to grab onto her if anything went wrong. I wanted her first lesson to be fun. If I could show her how to control her body's movement in the water rather than let the water control her, she could build from there. "It's healthy to fear the water, but you're going to show it you're the boss."

She slapped the surface. "Get it, water? I'm in charge here."

"That's right."

With each wave, water glided over the rocks and

drained into the pool, only to be sucked back with the current through channels between the enormous boulders.

I placed a hand on her back, lightly rubbing small circles between her shoulder blades.

Her muscles relaxed, and she leaned into my hand.

"I'm here for you. I won't let anything bad happen."

"What do I do now?"

Closing the distance between us, I slid my arm around her waist, my body pressed against hers. "First, you need to lean forward slightly, trusting the water to support you. Like this." I demonstrated, tilting my body to show her the position.

She followed suit, mimicking my movements tentatively. Her hair glistened with droplets of water, framing her face like dark tendrils. I resisted the urge to brush them away, focusing instead on teaching her.

"Kick your legs in a back-and-forth motion. You can also use your arms by spreading them wide and swirling them through the water. Both will keep you above the surface." I showed her by kicking my feet and moving the arm not around her, creating ripples in the pool.

She copied me, her legs flailing awkwardly at first but gradually finding a rhythm. Water splashed about as she gained confidence, her laughter mixing with the sound.

"That's it." I tightened my hold around her waist. "You're doing amazing."

We continued to practice, her embracing the water's buoyancy as I guided her movements. Each time she struggled or faltered, I offered words of encouragement and gentle adjustments. My hands trailed along her sides, providing both a steady presence and a subtle reassurance.

Her movements became more confident, as if she were born for this element.

"This is amazing." She tipped her head back and lifted her voice. "I love the water!" She splashed playfully, kicking up droplets that caught the muted light like falling stars. The crisp scent of the sea filled the air, and I couldn't stop grinning.

"You're advancing through this lesson faster than I expected," I said.

She huffed. "Did you think I couldn't do it?"

"I don't believe there's anything you can't do if you set your mind to it, Eleri." There was something undeniably beautiful about watching her conquer her worries and embrace this new experience. I grinned proudly, my heart swelling with love for this woman who'd become my everything.

I showed her a simple stroke she could use to propel herself through the water, and she floundered at first, quickly gaining competence as she glided from one end of the pool to the other.

Eventually, fatigue settled in. Sensing her muscles must feel heavy, I eased her back toward me. "Well done, mate. Hold on to me. It's time for you to rest."

Leaning back in my embrace, she sighed contentedly, her chest rising and falling in sync with mine.

"Thank you for teaching me," she murmured, her voice soft and tired.

I pressed a kiss to the top of her head and then her temple, savoring the taste of saltwater mixed with her skin. "It was my pleasure, my love. Always."

I lifted her out of the pool and onto the side, then joined her, our legs dangling like before.

As the cool breeze danced over my skin, I savored the moment, wrapped up in the afterglow of her accomplishment.

CHAPTER 22

ELERI

I'd never felt more alive in my life.

"The water's so buoyant," I said. "My leg doesn't hold me back when I'm floating or swimming." It had tired faster than the other, but if I kept practicing, would it grow stronger? "I'm going to swim every day until I'm the best swimmer on the island."

"You'll have a way to go to meet that, but I know you can do it." He smiled down at me.

I leaned against his side. To think that I was worried about mating with an orc. Instead, I'd found my other half, the one person who could complete me.

He kissed me again, and I climbed into his lap, pressing my body against his. Our skin was slick with water, and we slid together, the friction making heat channel through me.

What would it be like to be with him completely? I had a feeling I was going to find out soon.

With a groan, he laid me down on the rock and

continued to kiss me. It gave me the most amazing feeling. I'd only kissed one male, and his teeth were bad, and it tasted awful. Kissing Odik was like diving off a steep cliff or soaring through the air on the back of his vox.

His mouth grew urgent while his fingers roamed my body. He teased my nipples until they were ripe buds eager for his touch.

I wrapped my legs around him, holding tight, and a thrill shot through me when he pressed his stiff cock against my clit. He'd turned me into a demanding creature, but I sensed he'd give me everything I craved.

Leaving my mouth, he kissed down my neck, nibbling and biting, though not breaking the skin. Marking me as his own in a slow, simple way.

A moan wrenched from me, and when he looked up at me with hooded eyes, there wasn't anything I wouldn't do or give to make this male happy.

He kissed down to my breasts, and while one hand stroked one nipple, he ran his tusks across the other. He sucked it into his mouth, and each pull sent shockwaves through me. I'd never felt anything like this before and never dreamed such a wonderful feeling was possible.

Leaving my breast, he kissed down my belly. His tongue was hot and wet against my sensitive skin, making me arch into him and gasp in pleasure. His hands held me steady as he moved lower, spreading my legs apart.

He'd told me he was going to taste me there, and I couldn't wait to discover how it might feel.

My whole body thrummed with pleasure as he

explored, running circles around my clit with his tongue before finally dipping it inside me. I groaned at the scratchy feeling of his tongue running across my inner walls. He seemed to know exactly what I wanted, and I began to ride the wave of pleasure that was building inside me.

He began with gentle strokes that made me arch into him, then his tongue moved faster, stabbing inside me while he rolled my clit.

My fingers tangled in his hair before I latched onto his horns, holding tight, keeping his mouth where I needed him most. My mind spiraled. I couldn't believe how good it felt to be touched by him like this. He spread my legs wider, licking and sucking until I was trembling beneath him. His hands were everywhere—caressing my inner thighs, gripping my hips—and when I thought I couldn't take any more without shattering into a million pieces, he pressed two fingers inside me and stroked them in time with his mouth.

I came all at once, my cry of joy echoing around us.

His strokes slowed, and he looked up at me as his tongue made lazy circles around my still trembling clit.

When my body finally returned to the rocks, he was grinning.

"You taste wonderful. You, my mate, plus the sea. I'm going to need to suck on you at least once a day. You know that, right?"

My smile widened. I could barely think. Speaking was beyond me. I was still coming down from the wonderful sensation.

Rising, he lifted me into his arms.

"Our clothes," I said as he passed them.

"I'll return for them later. Right now, you're all that matters." With long strides, he carried me to the stairs. He kept going until he stood beside our bed.

"Mate," he said, all growly and possessive.

"Mate," I agreed.

"Unless you tell me to stop, I'm going to claim you."

"Don't stop," I whispered, pressing my face into his still-damp chest. "Never stop."

He lowered me onto the bed and followed. "That's all I need to hear."

My cock was on fire. I wanted her badly. But this was her first time, and I needed to make sure she was fully with me.

And my pendant. It lit up the night. This would be the last time I'd see the light from my clan's fates. Once I'd claimed my mate fully, it would no longer glow.

"There could be pain," I said.

"Don't worry about something like that," she said. "I imagine it's fleeting. Nothing."

"You tell me when you're ready." I kissed her again, savoring how amazing she felt naked beneath me. "I love you, mate," I said when I lifted my head.

"Odik." Tears sparkled in her eyes. "I love you too. Now show me everything I've been missing."

My heart soared all the way out to sea, spearing through the clouds looming over the island holding everything that mattered most. I'd love my mate. Protect her and any orclings the fates chose to give us. And treasure her always.

I kissed my way down her body, taking in the sweet smell of her skin, and reveling in the way she shivered beneath me. I paused at her breasts, exploring them with my tongue as I sucked each one into my mouth. She tasted like the sweetest fruit and smelled like a perfect summer day, and I wanted to savor every moment.

My hands roamed over her curves as I moved lower, feeling her heat calling out to me. With each stroke of my tongue, I could feel her desire growing. Her moans grew louder with each passing second until she was clinging and gasping.

Her fingers wrapped around my horns as I explored further with my mouth until she was shaking uncontrollably.

But just before she hit that sweet spot that would've sent her over the edge, I pulled away, leaving us both breathless.

Lifting her legs, I hitched them on my sides. She clung, her heels digging into my back, pulling me down to her.

Placing the head of my cock at her opening, I moved it through her wetness, stroking across her clit until she was panting and crying my name.

I was so much taller than her, but I arched my spine so I could meet her gaze as I shifted my hips forward, pushing the head of my cock inside her.

She bucked up toward me. "More. More!"

"All of me is yours, mate. All of me." With beads of sweat coiling down my brow, I pushed inside her further. She was so wet and tight. I was going to come within seconds, but I didn't want that. I needed to make sure she found pleasure first.

I rocked my hips, pushing slowly inside her, pulling back and driving harder each time until I was fully seated.

"How are you doing, mate?" I growled, barely able to maintain control. Her sheath sucked on my cock beautifully, and I wanted to pound into her until both of us exploded.

She stroked my arms, pulling me down. "More."

With a grin, I pulled out and plunged back inside her welcoming body.

My upper spur latched onto her clit and hummed, echoing the feeling growing inside me. The nubs on my cock vibrated, stroking her inner walls. The sensation shot through me as well, making my heat grow higher.

Her muscles tightened around my cock as I thrust faster. It was overwhelming, so intense.

"Odik," she cried, bucking up to meet each of my thrusts. "Yes. This. So much this."

My breathing grew heavy and ragged, as if the growing storm outside fused with me. Moving faster, I altered the depth of my thrusts and my pace, as she moaned and shifted beneath me.

With a cry, she came, her body convulsing beneath me, her passage tightening and releasing my cock.

Moving faster, I gave in, letting my body take over.

My orgasm crashed through me, and I cried out, shuddering as my cock jerked tight, shooting my seed inside her.

CHAPTER 24
ELERI

I woke beside my mate. My love. A grin rose on my face. What we'd done last night . . .

Well, I wanted him to do it again. I'd never imagined two bodies could give each other such pleasure.

His arms tightened around me where I lay on his chest, and he kissed the top of my head gently.

Rising over him, I smiled. "Hey, mate."

"Hey to you too, mate."

I shifted up until I could kiss him, marveling all over again at how wonderful it was just to be with him.

His fingertips traced up and down my sides, and it wasn't long before one of his hands slipped between my legs.

"Wet," he growled. "Incredibly wet."

"I want to try something," I said, straddling his waist.

"Walk along the shore? Swim in the sea? I know. You want to cook me some fish."

Tease.

"No, this." Taking his cock, I ran my fingers up and down it. "What do these nubs on the sides do?"

"I believe you discovered that last night when they moved within you. They vibrate."

"And this?" I stroked the smaller cock mounted above the larger one.

A quiver went through him.

"It likes to be touched," I said, gripping it in my palm and milking it like my body would if it was embedded inside me.

"Even more, it likes sucking on your clit while I ride you."

"This morning, I want to ride you."

His eyes widened, as did his grin. "You can ride me whenever you want, mate."

Just the thought of it made me wetter. Rising over him, I placed the head of his cock at my opening. There had been a small sting when he pushed inside me last night, but I suspected that would be the last time it would hurt.

Now his big, thick cock would only give me pleasure.

I lowered my body down, but despite stretching me, I couldn't get him all the way inside.

"Slowly, mate," he said with a growl, his body trembling. "Lift and drop down again. Keep pressing, and I suspect you'll find what you need. What we both need."

I slowly rocked my hips, pressing down and lifting

up. With each movement, I felt myself opening wider in anticipation. His body was warm, and each time I moved down, he shifted his hips up to meet me.

Slowly, my body opened, and he was finally able to slide in all the way. The sensation of being filled completely by him was nearly overwhelming. It left me gasping for air.

Lifting his upper body, he cupped my face with his hands and brought his lips close to mine.

"You feel wonderful," he murmured before pressing a kiss onto my lips. His eyes were full of love as he laid back and looked at me. My smile made my cheeks ache.

I started to move up and down on him.

He groaned beneath me as I moved faster, each drop of my body bringing us closer together until we were both panting heavily. His hands roamed over my chest and hips while I rode him harder, delighting in how it felt when he stroked my nipples.

His upper spur kept hitting my clit and when it latched on and started humming, my eyeballs rolled back in my head. My moan was deep and guttural.

As if he sensed my leg had started to ache, his hands landed on my hips. He guided my movements as we both increased our pace, driving each other closer to the explosion.

The heat built inside me until it was too much to bear.

I cried out as an orgasm roared over me like a heavy wave crashing against the shoreline. He followed soon after with a deep groan that sent shivers through me.

I collapsed on his chest, and he stroked my back, whispering nonsense words that meant the world to me.

"You, my mate, are perfect," he growled. "You thrill me like no other. I'll treasure you for the rest of my days."

And that was when I knew I'd love him until my dying day.

After breakfast, we placed the fish in totes and distributed it to our clan.

"Thank you," an elderly orc female, Madine, said when we handed her a generous share of our catch. Her gaze fell on me, and she gave me a tusk-filled grin. "Nice of you to bring your new mate by, Caedos." She patted my arm. "You're the first human I've met, but I suspect you won't be the last. Welcome."

I spontaneously gave her a hug, and while she grunted, her smile held true when I stepped back once more. "It's nice to meet you too."

"Go on with you two," she said, her face darkening. "I've got fish to place in my cool box, enough to tide me over the storm. You two have more fish to deliver. Do stop by soon, though, and we'll share stories." Her gaze met mine. "I would love to hear some of the older tales from the village where you grew up."

"I'd love to share them," I said. "Maybe you have some stories you can share about Odik."

I grinned when he groaned.

"Bring him, too." Madine playfully elbowed Odik's

side. "I'll let him listen. He needs to hear some of the older tales again."

"Madine's the keeper of our past." Odik tapped his temple. "She has all the clan history locked in her mind."

"You know I hope to find someone to pass the stories on to." Tilting her head, she studied me. "I'm still searching for one special person." Her hands lifted and dropped to her sides. "Anyway. I'm sure you have others to visit. Thank you for stopping by to share a bit of time with an old lady."

"Anytime." Odik gently kissed her temple, and we stepped outside her tidy home. "I'll stop by when the tempest is over. I made sure you have enough wood to keep your home warm." He strode over to a shed attached to the side of her tidy house and peered inside. "Plenty." He carried three loads into her house, placing them in the bin beside her stove.

"You shouldn't worry about me, Caedos," she said, patting my arm. "You as well, Eleri. Thank you both."

He braced her shoulders and stared into her eyes. "You know I'll do anything for you. Please don't hesitate to ask if you have need."

We left her, carrying the totes into the main part of the village, though it was only six homes clustered together.

Trilden jumped when we walked up behind him, turning from a cart loaded with various items and hitched to a creature much like the beasts of burden my human village used for travel.

"Would you like help?" Odik asked. "I'd offer fish, but I'm sure you've already stocked your cold chest."

"Oh, no. I, er, don't need help." Trilden's face darkened, but I suspected he wasn't embarrassed about being offered help like Madine. "Thank you though." His voice went blustery. "I'll, um, see you in a bit." He rushed inside the nearby building.

Odik frowned and stared at the items in the cart. Two bags filled with what looked like clothing, a cold box that appeared unearthed from the ground if the dirt on the outside was anything to go by, and wooden furniture were tied to the cart.

The devastation on Odik's face hit me in the chest like a hammer. "He's . . ." He strode to the house and stepped inside. I followed, entering the tidy living area almost empty of furniture. "Trilden?" Odik continued to the small kitchen along the back right wall where his friend stood with his back to us, loading items into a wooden crate. "You're leaving too?"

"Just for the tempest," Trilden said, not turning to face Odik. "I'm sure I'll be back."

"When? After the storm or . . ." Odik sucked in a deep breath and released it with a sigh. "Or when you're too old to care about working any longer?"

"It's nothing you've done, Odik," Trilden said softly, finally facing his caedos. "But there are more opportunities in the city. We're half-starving here. You know that. Frankly, you should consider moving as well."

"What would I do in the city?"

"Whatever the rest of us will do. Take a job making

steel panels for the buildings. Fight off the dresalods. Or travel far into the mountains where the storms won't reach us."

"I can't control the sky or the sea." Defeat tinged Odik's voice, and I wanted to wrap my arms around him and tell him everything would be alright. But I couldn't fix this.

"You're the best caedos this clan has seen." The honesty in Trilden's voice made me ache for both males. "If there was a way to increase crop growth, to bring livestock who could survive drinking salt water, I'd not only stay, but I'd recruit others to move here from the mainland. But we rely too heavily on inconsistent rain for anything like that."

Odik drew himself up stiffly. "I understand. Know we'll welcome you back if you change your mind."

"Thank you, friend." With that, Trilden turned back to his packing.

As he passed me, Odik took my hand, leading me from the small home.

"At this rate, we'll soon be alone on the island." He said nothing further as we distributed the rest of the fish to the villagers. He also said nothing as we walked home with our empty totes.

His steps were slow. He must feel as if the weight of the entire world rested on his shoulders.

CHAPTER 25

ODIK

As I made sure our home could withstand the tempest, I did all I could to remove the idea of Trilden leaving from my mind. How many did that leave on the island now? I didn't need to count in my mind. Three left the day my mate arrived. Now Trilden. Just twenty-six. How long until only me, my mate, and Madine remained?

When I entered our home, Eleri greeted me with a smile. "I've prepared a good meal for you, mate." She gestured to the table.

It almost broke me to see she'd prepared my favorite dish. A small jar holding a scant bit of water and flowers sat in the center of the table.

"Eleri," I groaned, lifting her up for a kiss that went on so long, I contemplated taking her to the bedroom before we ate. No, where I could eat her. But she'd worked hard to prepare something she thought would make me happy, and I wanted to savor each bite.

She slid down my front and sashayed over to the table, sending me a shy smile. "I collected wild greens to go with the meal and found some tubers I roasted in butter you keep in the cool box. I assume that comes from the mainland?"

"As Trilden pointed out, we don't have enough fresh water to keep milk-producing beasts to make our own butter."

"If we had more water, would we have enough land to support them?"

"Definitely. Despite our crops not growing well, we've maintained a balance of open fields and forest."

"Why do you do that when you don't have enough water?"

"Sometimes, we see frequent rain. Then our crops flourish. We're always prepared for it to happen."

We sat, and I dug in, groaning at how wonderfully she'd seasoned the fish.

"I used herbs I collected in the woods beside the house," she said with a smile. "I suspect this land has everything we need to sustain life for many more than the few who choose to live here."

"If only it rained enough to keep our barrels full all the time."

Her smile widened. "It's raining now and that will refill the barrels. We can bathe in salt water."

"And boil it for drinking water."

Her head tilted. "We don't drink the rainwater?"

"We can, though we save most of it for our crops. If you boil salt water and collect the steam, it's fresh and drinkable. Boiling leaves the salt behind in the pan." I gestured to the small container on the table. "We then use the salt to season our food."

"Is it possible to boil and collect enough clean water to feed a huge field of crops?"

I shook my head. "We've tried it with large kettles and big open fires, but it's an incredible amount of work. Too much work when so few people live on the island."

"I wish there was a way to make this possible for everyone. Then you could recruit people to live here with us. We need to grow the population to a level that will provide the services we all need to share our best lives."

"I wish that was possible too, but it isn't. The life you see here is fading faster than I ever thought possible. When my father took over the clan, there were over one hundred living on the island. Now we're just twenty-six."

"Twenty-seven."

I frowned.

"Don't forget me, love."

"Ah, you're right." This time, my smile was true. Being with Eleri made everything better. "If only the Mate Hunt ran each month. We could bring woman to the island and match them with our males. Then our population would go up instead of down."

"I'm not giving up yet."

And I appreciated that. I took her hand lying on the table beside her plate and squeezed it. "Thank you."

"For what?"

I gestured to my food. "This excellent meal. And for being here with me. For listening and loving me."

"There's no place I'd rather be and no one I'd rather be with."

We ate, savoring the meal, then cleaned the dishes together in the sink.

After, I leaned against the counter, watching as Eleri puttered around the living area, tidying things that truly didn't need tidying.

The wind howled around my snug home, seeking entrance it wouldn't find. I expected the full force of the storm to hit just past midnight.

"I believe I owe you a song and a dance," I said.

She stopped and turned my way, a throw pillow held against her body. "Remember, I've never danced."

I stepped toward her. "Then it's time you did, my love."

"My leg may hold me back."

Taking the pillow from her, I tossed it onto the sofa and tugged her into my arms. "If it hurts, tell me, and we'll stop." To make sure it wouldn't ache, I lifted her. This also put us at eye level, which meant I could give her a quick kiss.

She moaned and clung to my shoulders.

Lifting my head, I grinned with happiness. "I believe I mentioned something about singing as well?"

"If I know the tune, I'll hum it for you."

"How about this one?" I started a robust song about females with skirts swirling about their ankles and a male's intention to seduce her.

Eleri laughed as I twirled her around the small space

between the kitchen and living area, her head tilted back, and her hair swishing across her back.

My life may be getting harder, and only the fates knew what the future had in store for my clan, but as long as I held Eleri, I could smile.

CHAPTER 26
ELERI

We danced and sang well into the evening, laughing until our voices began to croak and Odik's legs must've ached from spinning me around.

Our happiness shoved the lingering sadness out the door. It could wallow in the storm instead of tainting the joy we found with each other inside our snug home.

Wiped out, we collapsed on the sofa, where I leaned against his side. His arm went around me, and he kissed the top of my head.

"There's no one I'd rather weather a storm with than you, mate," he said.

I was grateful to hear joy in his voice. He'd felt fragile earlier, which was why I put so much effort into our meal. There wasn't much I could do to cheer him up, but simple things often worked better than anything else.

Knowing you were loved helped the most.

"I love you," I said, lifting my voice to be heard above the storm.

"Mate." He lifted me up to sit on his lap, facing him, and kissed me.

I snuggled into his embrace while the storm raged around us.

"Is it a good time to go down to the rocks to watch the storm?" I asked.

"We'll go tomorrow, when it has passed, and the tide has retreated. It'll be safe then. That's also a good time to collect wood the storm leaves on the shore. I gather it into a sizeable pile near the base of the cliff and use it to light a fire when I camp on the shore."

"Camping?"

"Sleeping outside with only the stars as my roof."

"Do bugs nibble?"

His arms tightened around me. "Only mates who are eager to be with the one they love."

I couldn't stop grinning. He said all the right things, but to him, they were more than words. They were feelings spoken from deep within his heart, and they touched me in a way nothing and no one else ever had.

A gust of wind slammed into the side of the building, but it didn't budge.

"A distant grandfather built this home, and each generation has improved it," he said. "You're safe here."

"I'm safe anywhere when your arms are around me."

"Can you feel the storm?"

I closed my eyes. "The atmosphere crackles with electricity, as if the very air pulses with raw power."

With every flash of lightning illuminating the room, shadows danced across the walls, casting eerie shapes on the furniture.

"Can you feel the tension coiling in your chest?" he asked, taking me with him on a journey to explore the sensations generated by the storm. "This isn't just any storm—it's an enormous tempest. A beast sent from the sky."

I found myself both captivated and apprehensive about what lay ahead. Our home was tight and well-built, but the storm sounded ferocious, a vicious creature determined to find its way inside to defeat us.

A rumble of thunder rang out, resonating deep within my bones and shaking the house.

"It's a chorus to nature," I whispered. "One of chaos, power, and awe." Rain battered the windows relentlessly, as if it sought to breach our sanctuary at the top of the rocky cliff. "Does anyone ever go outside during a storm like this?"

"I have. Remember? My father used to take me down to the rocks."

"You said once the storm had mostly passed."

"We could try to go outside right now if you want."

"Really?"

"Really."

"Let's do it." I couldn't wait to face the force battering our home. We wouldn't do anything unsafe, but maybe he meant we could peek out the door.

He rose with me sheltered in his arms and walked down the hallway. A door at the end led outside to a room with a solid roof and screened walls. The room wound partly around to the side facing the sea.

"Why didn't I see this here?" I shouted to be heard above the wind.

With a shrug, Odik sat in the solitary chair facing the water. "I don't use the room often, though I should."

Despite the chair being placed against the inner wall, raindrops pattered on the floor, splashing my lower legs exposed by my skirt. I'd long since kicked off my shoes, and there was something exhilarating about letting the storm touch my toes in this way.

Slipping from his lap, I approached the outer wall and clung to the railing, peering through the screen at the sea churning far below.

Odik came up behind me and I leaned back into his embrace, secure despite the tempest trying to claim victory over our souls.

The salty scent of the ocean hit my senses, and the tang of brine filled my nose, intermingling with the crisp sweetness of wet earth. Below, the waves surged with ferocity, crashing against the cliffs with a deafening roar. A fine mist rose, caught by the wind and carried toward us.

Feeling invigorated and alive, I trembled with a mixture of fear and excitement. One moment, the world around would vanish beneath an inky shroud, swallowed by the blackness of the storm; the next, a bolt of lightning would crackle across the sky, tracing jagged paths through the stars and lighting up everything around us.

The trees creaked and groaned, gusts of wind wrapping around them and sucking at their leaves. Our tiny house held firm, defying the storm safely amid chaos.

Time passed like an adrenaline-fueled blur, and soon we were soaked through. I shivered, partly from the cold but also from the energy released by the storm.

"You're cold," Odik said. "And wet."

I grinned at him. "You're wet too. Why don't we go inside and warm each other up?"

"I like how you think, mate."

He swept me up in his arms and strode into the house, kicking the door closed behind him.

In our bedroom, he gently removed my clothing and his own.

Then he replaced his fingers on my skin with his mouth.

CHAPTER 27

ELERI

I woke during the night to complete silence. No drumming of rain on the roof, and no wind gusting against the shutters barring our windows, trying to find a way in. The storm was over. With a grin, I snuggled into my husband's side. He murmured something, kissing the top of my head as his arms wrapped around me. I drifted back to sleep.

When I woke again, morning sunlight streamed in through the window on my left. Odik must've gotten up sometime and removed the shutters.

"We made it," I said. Reaching out, I found Odik gone. But the smell of food cooking and his low whistled tune tugged me from our bed and down the hall—with a quick stop in the bathroom and to tug on a nightie. I entered our tiny kitchen where he prepared breakfast at the stove. He continued whistling the same song he'd sang last night, shifting his hips along with the tune.

"Have a seat, lovely one," he called over his shoulder,

adding a grin. "I'm going to serve you a meal unlike any other."

"It smells wonderful." I dropped into the chair, smiling at how my feet dangled. Everything in the house was orc-sized, which meant it was much too big for me. I felt a bit like I lived in a doll's house, though no dollhouse ever held Odik. He told me he was going to make me some smaller furniture, and I loved that he'd do that for me.

"Tea," he said, lowering a mug in front of me. "I collect the herbs on the island, and this is my special blend."

"I didn't know you were a tea connoisseur." Lifting the cup, I closed my eyes and took a sniff. "I smell hints of vanilla."

"I pick the beans, preserve them, and grate some into the mix."

"And aspest berries."

"Good catch. They also grow on the island. I dry them and add a few to each pot."

"And . . . weelen leaves?"

"Yes, that's the main leaf in the mix."

I took a sip, moaning at how delicious it tasted. "It's perfect."

"I was hoping you'd like it. I made a big pot, and we can share it while we enjoy our breakfast." He placed a heaping plate in front of me, the other on the opposite side of the table. Sitting, he waved his eating implement my way. "I might've overcooked."

"We worked up an appetite."

His smile joined in with mine. "That we did."

"What's on the agenda today?" I asked as I bit into the thick slice of bread he'd toasted and covered with mellabar jam. My belly roared its approval.

"Lots of clean-up. I want to check on everyone first, however."

"Why don't I stay here and start collecting brush and whatever else the storm has left behind? You can travel faster without me."

"Alright." He ate a slice of brugel meat, and I did the same, savoring the crispy, salty treat. "I should only need the morning. That's where it pays to make sure everyone's ready for a tempest. Madine will need the most help. She's the oldest—and savviest—person on the island. I'll clean up her yard, and if I know her, she'll invite me for lunch, so don't wait for me for that. I should be back by mid-afternoon."

"If I run out of things to do around the house, I'll go down to the beach and collect driftwood. I'll stack it near the cliffs like you suggested."

"Don't go close to the water. The sea's often turbulent for a while after a storm and an unexpected wave could grab you."

I nodded and placed a piece of brugel meat between a folded slice of toast, making a small sandwich.

I couldn't finish my meal, but when I shoved the plate closer to Odik, he had no problem cleaning my plate after doing the same with his own. At nearly twice my size, he needed more food than me.

"I wonder how the garden fared," I said. "I'll check on that too."

"At least it's been watered."

"I'll cover the barrels to keep out bugs."

"Thank you." He took my hand across the table and squeezed it. "You're amazing, mate. I don't know where I'd be without you."

"Same, Odik. Same."

"In a few days, once the sea has calmed, let's go to the city. We can pick up sewing supplies and fabric for you, and you can sew till your heart's content."

"That would be wonderful. Thanks."

"While we're there, we'll have lunch. There are nice restaurants in the city."

"Are there any on the island?"

"Not any longer. The chef who ran one left over a year ago. She runs a new establishment in the city now, and we can stop by to introduce you." His smile held a hint of sadness. "I keep hoping I can talk her into returning to the island, but at this point, there'd be almost no customers. I don't blame her for leaving. I don't blame *anyone*, for that matter."

"We'll find a way to bring people here, even if we have to kidnap them to show them the beauty of this way of life."

He chuckled. "No kidnapping allowed. But I love that you enjoy it here as much as me."

"It's our home, and it always will be. We'll raise our orclings here." When his eyes lit up, I laughed. "I don't know if I'm pregnant yet, but it's not for a lack of trying."

"There's nothing I'd love more than to see you holding our child."

The love in his voice gutted me. "I can't wait."

"May the fates bless us."

After he left, I went outside and tackled the downed branches, dragging them into a pile near the shed where he stored our wood for winter beneath the overhang. The sticks and branches would make great kindling. It didn't get horribly cold in this part of the world, but we were far from shore. I was sure the dampness set into your bones and made you shiver. A fire would be welcome, and I'd noted the small stove in the living area. We could sit on the sofa and enjoy it.

Maybe while snuggling our child.

"That's far in the future and only if the fates gift us," I said to myself as I dragged another branch over to the growing pile.

I was lifting the last branch when someone came up behind me. Thinking Odik had forgotten something, I turned.

My smile fell immediately. "Drabass."

"Eleri." His grin came out more like a leer.

"Odik's in the house. Let me get him for you."

"I saw him on the path leading to the village. Nice of you to offer, however." He stepped closer to me. "I don't believe we need him, do we?"

I spun and bolted for the house, but he leaped and

dragged us both to the ground, rolling until I was beneath him.

When he tried to kiss me, I snapped my head to the side, smacking his shoulders.

He growled and pinned my hands over my head. I shrieked and grabbed a nearby rock, smacking him with it.

He was wrenched off me.

Odik snarled and punched Drabass in the nose. Green blood gushed, and Drabass howled, cupping his face.

I scrambled to my feet and backed away, holding the rock so tight in my hand, it made my fingers sting.

Odik's punch in Drabass's belly was followed by him slamming his clenched fists down on top of Drabass's head. The orc slumped to the ground and didn't move.

I dropped the rock and it thudded on the ground beside my foot.

Odik rushed over to me and lifted me gently. "Are you alright?"

"I am. He . . . He just got here."

"I'm glad I decided to turn back. I forgot to bring more fish for Madine."

I didn't want to think about what might've happened if he hadn't returned. Would he have stopped if I hit him hard enough with the rock? I would've tried.

"I'll take you inside."

I clung to his shoulders. "I can stay here."

"I'd feel better if you were locked inside the house."

"But I can't stay there forever. It's no better than

hiding behind the fortress walls back at the village." And I'd already seen nowhere was safe. "I want to keep working."

He cupped my face and stared into my eyes. "You're sure?"

"I am." My voice might tremble, but my will did not.

"I need to take care of Drabass."

My breath caught. "What will you do with him?"

"What all orcs do with someone who harms a female." His grim gaze met mine. "All you need to know is that he won't bother you again."

"Will you send him to the city?"

"We can't take the chance he'll do this to someone else."

I had no sympathy for Drabass, but this sounded like a harsh punishment.

If I was going to fit in with this life, I had to accept orc ways. Odik was right. It would be better if I didn't ask any more questions.

"You're sure?" he asked.

I looked around at all that needed to be done and stiffened my spine, nodding.

He left, returning half an hour later. "I took him to his father and explained. Crickin will handle it now."

"What will he do?"

His gaze met mine. "You don't want to know."

Drabass didn't deserve my sympathy, so I grunted.

"Come with me into town," Orik said, taking my hands and squeezing them.

I wanted to cling so much, but I also wanted to stand

strong. "There's a lot left to do still, and I'm going to keep working."

If I was going to be an orc's mate, that also meant I needed to bravely face whatever this life handed me. Not being accosted by one of the orcs but doing my share as the caedos's wife.

"I'll stay here and finish."

"I feel bad that it happened."

"You didn't do it. You saved me, Odik."

He tugged me into his arms. "I'll always be here for you, mate."

We sat together for a bit before he left, telling me to lock the door and remain inside.

I couldn't do it. My life was here, and I was going to grab onto it fully. So I faced my fear and went back outside.

Once I'd finished cleaning up the yard, I walked through the woods to the garden, finding the plants flatter than I'd like but still green. The rain would serve them well; the ground was very parched before the storm.

My hands no longer shook, and I was proud of myself for facing this head on, of making something good come from what was almost a shitty day.

I picked vegetables and brought them to the house, then went back out to cover all the full rain barrels. I also re-mulched the garden to hold the moisture.

After, I sat in the kitchen and ate, surprised I had an appetite after what happened. Hard work and sunshine would do that to you.

That and knowing Odik would always be here for me.

I put everything away and washed the dishes I'd neglected after breakfast. Then I went out to look down over the rail.

"Tons of driftwood." The beach was littered with it, dry gray bones from long-dead trees.

I drank a glass of water and took the stairs to the beach, proud of all I'd accomplished so far. Odik was going to be pleased when he returned to our tidy home and saw there wasn't anything left for him to do.

Throughout the afternoon, I collected driftwood, piling it near the cliff.

"Where did you come from?" I asked one of the pieces. "And how far did you travel?" For all I knew, it had made its way to the island from the mainland. Or maybe from one of the other uninhabited islands.

Finished, I surveyed the wood I'd stacked in big piles. We had enough for many fires on the shore. Perhaps we could cook fish on the flames one night. On sticks? I wasn't sure how it might be done. I'd only had fish a few times while living in the village. It was much too rare and costly for someone like me.

I was wiping my hands on my skirt when something glinting at the point drew my attention. Assuming it must be a shiny rock or piece of random metal like the other refuse I'd collected in a separate pile near the driftwood, I strode in that direction.

Just like I'd thought. I lifted the hunk of metal, wondering where *it* might've come from. The mainland for sure, or perhaps a ship lost at sea if anyone plied ships in this area.

Turning to head back with the plan of scaling the stairs and getting cleaned up before Odik returned, I frowned. I stopped and stared toward the small, recessed area I'd remarked on the other day.

The surge of water had washed away at the cliff, scooping sand and rocks out of the depression. In fact, from where I stood, it looked like there *was* a cave there now.

"Huh," I mumbled, walking toward it, passing the pool where I'd started to learn to swim.

When I reached the area, my eyes widened.

The storm had changed things. Now, it *was* a cave, and it went in farther than I could see.

I'd find Odik and tell him.

We could return together later and explore it.

CHAPTER 28
ODIK

"I'm home," I called out when I reached our small cabin.

There was nothing better than knowing that I wouldn't return to an empty house. My mate might not be waiting, but she'd be nearby.

My weary soul needed her comfort and presence as much as she probably needed me. I hadn't wanted to leave her earlier after what happened, but I'd seen the resolution in her eyes. She wanted to face the aftermath alone, and it was a wise idea. I couldn't always be with her, and she needed to feel confident, not scared, when she was alone.

I'd teach her how to use a blade, however. It was incredibly rare for a male to attack a female, though not unheard of. We treasured our women; no one would dream of taking advantage of them.

Yet he had.

His father would make sure it never happened to

another female again, and I wouldn't ask him what he'd done. That was for him as the head of his family to decide.

I sighed as I heeled off my boots. Three more islanders were leaving, bringing us down to twenty-four. At this rate, we'd be living with only Madine for company. She was a sweet woman, but I hated how my clan was fading away and there wasn't anything I could do about it.

Even the heavy rain didn't convince those leaving to stay. *It'll dry out again,* they said. *But there's still nothing left for us here.*

Our hearts were here—that's what was left. But they didn't see it my way.

When Eleri didn't reply, I went looking for her. I admired the sizable pile of branches she'd collected in a pile near the woods, plus the uncluttered area surrounding our home.

I also didn't find her in the garden or near any of the barrels. The beach, then?

When I started down the stairs, I found her climbing toward me and waited for her to join me.

"You're back," she exclaimed, giving me a hug.

I kissed her, savoring how wonderful she felt in my arms.

"How did everyone do with the storm?" she asked, leaning back to look up at me.

"They all fared well." I'd share about those leaving later. "How did everything go for you?"

"Very well." Her smile came easy, and her eyes gleamed with happiness. "I battled my fears and won."

"I'm proud of you, mate."

She nodded pertly. "What were you up to while you were gone?"

"I cleaned up Madine's yard, stacking the wood near her shed like you did here. There wasn't as much in the center of the island where she lives, but she was grateful for the help."

"Let's have her over at our place soon. We can bring her down to the beach and build a big fire with the driftwood I collected. We'll cook fish and listen to the waves."

One of my favorite things to do. "That's a great idea. I doubt Madine gets to the beach often. I can carry her down and back, and I bet if we asked, she'll tell us stories about those who lived here long ago while we sit by the fire after our meal."

"Tales of your past. That would be amazing."

"We can learn so much from those who came before us." I tapped my temple. "And Madine remembers them all."

"Who'll learn the stories from her to carry them forward?"

"I've done what I can to memorize some, but it's one of many tasks I feel I can't complete as well as I'd like." It made me sad to think some stories would be lost when she passed, but hopefully, if I could lure people to the island, one of them would sit and listen to her tales until they knew them by heart. Then, the tales would continue on as they should.

"I found something exciting," Eleri said, taking my hand and urging me down the stairs. She led me across the beach, and I marveled at what she'd gotten done. All I'd accomplished was stacking some wood, eating with Madine, and pretty much begging my clansmales not to leave the island. They reluctantly said they'd wait two days before giving me their final answer, but they'd continued packing. The sea was too rough for them to travel—for now.

"What is it?" I asked, as she led me across the beach to the point. "Is the swimming hole still there?"

She frowned at me. "It's surrounded by rock. I doubt even the strongest storm could destroy it."

"We can swim tomorrow if you'd like."

She nodded. "Let's. But for today . . ."

We walked around the point and toward the pool.

"Look." She stopped; her arm lifted.

I stared toward the cliff. "Wow."

"The storm must've eaten into the cliff. I wonder if there was a cave there long ago, and maybe a different tempest filled it in with sand and rock."

I squeezed her hand. "Did you go inside?"

"I wanted to do that with you." She grinned but a tiny shiver shot through her. "There could be beasts hiding inside."

She wasn't far off with her suggestion. The dresalods wouldn't leave the water as long as it churned, but within days, we'd have to watch for their next attack. Since they hated the sun, they rarely attacked during the day and only then when the water was calm. One good thing about tempests.

For now, we were safe on the beach. One day, we'd have to find a permanent solution to them, but I couldn't imagine what that might be.

We walked closer to the cave.

"Should I wait out here?" she asked.

I scanned the sea but saw nothing of concern.

"Come with me," I said. "I doubt there's anything to be worried about inside the cave, and we can explore it together."

"Maybe there's a long-lost treasure inside."

I grinned and tugged her against my side as we walked in that direction. "I doubt it. I'm sure you're about to be disappointed."

"If it's nothing but a shallow cave, we'll return to our home." She shot me a sultry look. "I missed you today. We need to make up for the time we were apart."

I loved that she craved me as much as I did her. As with all true matings like ours, it would only get better as we aged.

It was dark inside the cave, so dark, we stumbled over something lying across the sandy floor.

"Wait here," I said. "I'll go grab a light."

I was back before she could miss me, though I caught her shivering in the low light when I approached. She gazed at the pool and leaped toward me when I came closer.

"Something splashed in the water," she said.

"Sometimes fish are washed in during a storm. A bonus for us because they're easy to catch."

"It's a good thing I enjoy fish."

"Let's check out this cave, then, shall we?" I held up the light, and we walked deeper inside. The narrow area widened, and we entered a large room with a roof a few feet higher than the top of my head. Small pools peppered the floor and—

"What's that?" Eleri asked, pointing to big object near the back wall.

"I don't know."

"The sea didn't construct them."

She was right. Orcs must've. Or humans, though I didn't believe any had ever lived on the island. "They look carved from stone."

We stopped beside the largest structure, staring at the water rising all the way to the brim.

"It looks like a tub," Eleri said. "Would high tide reach this area? Oh, I know the answer to that. It wouldn't or it would've exposed the cave earlier."

Water trickled along a channel spanning the right wall, and the channel was tilted just enough to keep the water moving until it dumped into the tub.

"We could bathe here," she said, dipping her fingertip into the water. "Salty, of course, but it's not any different from the pool."

"But it is." I frowned at the structures, trying to determine what they might be, while Eleri strolled around the room.

"Look," she said, pointing at drawings on the wall.

"Someone built this, and I think the markings show us what it might be." Moving closer, she traced her fingertip from one drawing to another. "It looks like water is channeled from the sea at high tide. It flows like it's doing now until it fills the tub." She shot me a grin. "It's like the plumbing I heard they have in a distant village to bring water from the river into a home. You can fill a tub or have a drink at the sink. Can you imagine?"

If only I could do something like this for my mate. Life on the island was enough of a burden without worrying about how we'd find water to bathe and drink.

Eleri leaned closer to the wall. "It looks like they filter the water as it travels from the sea. And the filter allows the refuse to drop below the channel, keeping it out of the fresher water. Why would they do something like that?" Leaving the drawings, she meandered around the cave, studying the structure while I approached the markings, wondering if I could see what she hadn't.

"Interesting," she said, pointing to a structure mounted above the pool. "It looks like a hood. And there's a hole in the top. Look. They built that from metal, and it slopes downward from the hood and into a second pool. This is a very odd thing." Tilting her head, she scanned the structure. "There's piping beneath the second pool that . . . If I didn't know better, I'd think it channels water someplace else, but where?" She stooped down and peered beneath the first pool. "The stone beneath the first pool has scorch marks like they lit a fire here. But why?"

A fire . . .

Something wild occurred to me, and I rushed over to confirm my suspicion.

It didn't take long, and soon, I was shaking my head and grinning. I picked Eleri up and spun her around, my laughter bursting free. She joined in, though from the puzzlement on her face, it was clear she had no idea why I was suddenly happy.

"I think, my love, you've found it," I finally said.

"Found what?"

"The desalinization device Madine once mentioned in one of her stories."

ELERI

"A desalinization device?" I asked, excitement making my feet jump on the sandy floor.

"From many generations ago. I don't know why they stopped using it. Maybe the sea buried it, and it was too much work to clean out."

"Or only a few knew about it? Almost anything could've happened."

"It became the stuff of legends, part of a broader story Madine would tell us. My father scoffed at the idea and told me we'd collected rainwater forever and that was good enough. But without water, we can't maintain life here, let alone grow our population."

"We should tell everyone," I said. Maybe then we'd bring people to the island instead of sadly watching them leave.

"Let's see if we can get the device working first." He frowned as he studied each component, paying a lot of attention to the piping that left the last vat on the right.

"What should we do?" Returning to the drawings on the wall, I tapped my finger on the first. "We've got water in the biggest tub, and it shows a fire beneath it."

"As you know, we boil water and collect the condensation to drink, leaving salt behind in the pan. This is the same theory only on a larger scale."

"I'll go get some of the wood I collected, and we'll see if this baby works. If it doesn't, we won't disappoint anyone." Except ourselves. I couldn't imagine how wonderful it might be to have clear water all year round regardless of whether it rained or not.

"I'll get wood," he said. "Would you collect dry seaweed?"

"Sure."

Outside, he loaded his arms with wood and carried it inside while I collected seaweed kindling.

We lit a fire beneath the biggest tub and stood back to watch what happened. It took some time, and lots of wood burned, but the water started steaming. The steam rose up into the hood over the tub and the trickle of water rang out as the condensation made its way down the metal pipe.

"It's dripping into the second tub," Odik shouted. He swooped me up and spun me around, giving me a big kiss before he placed my feet back on the sand. "It's working. It's working!"

"Let's test it." I went over to watch the condensation continue dripping, very slowly filling the second container.

Odik dipped his hand into the water and took a sip. He grinned my way. "It's not salty."

"Amazing. We can set up a system where we bring buckets of water from here to the surface."

"I want to talk to Madine. One of her stories may contain another clue to what our ancestors did with the water. Carrying buckets is a lot of work, though I'll do it rather than go without."

"The water's half gone from the first tub," I pointed out.

"Then let's refill it." Odik cranked a handle on the wall near the tub, and water started gushing in from the sea, channeled through piping in the wall.

"This is ingenious. I can't believe it was lost to your people."

"*Our* people, mate." He put his arm around me and kissed the top of my head. "This belongs to all of us."

We loaded more wood beneath the cooking vat and returned to the top of the island. Not stopping, we rushed to the village, where we found orcs loading carts with their things.

"Ten," Odik said in shock. He came to a stop and stared in dismay at his friends packing up to leave. "I thought three more were leaving, but never this many."

"We've got to stop them." I hurried forward, slowing before I reached them.

Trilden looked up from where he was tying a sack to his cart. "You can't say anything that'll change our minds. We can't live like this. The city will give us a decent life."

"It won't be anything like the life you've had on the island," Odik said.

"Sometimes a male has to give up things he loves to survive."

"You don't have to leave," I said.

One of the males frowned, his hands stilling on chair he'd just loaded onto his cart.

"We found a way to create lots of clean water," Odik said. "Actually, my mate discovered a way." He tugged me against his side, putting his arm around my shoulders.

"That's not possible," Trilden said. "Believe me, if it was, I'd unload everything right now."

"Then you'd better start unloading. Odik would never give anyone false hope." We turned to find Madine joining us, moving slowly with the support of her cane. She looked between me and Odik. "What have you found?"

"Remember the story about our clan having more fresh water than we knew what to do with?" Odik asked.

"A story?" Trilden grumbled. "You think to hold us here with a tale?"

"Not every story is made up," Madine said, stiffening. "Many tell of things in our past we don't want to forget."

"Eleri and I have found a way to remove the salt from sea water," Odik said.

"We do this already." Trilden braced Odik's shoulders. "You've been an amazing caedos. The best this clan has seen in ages. No one cares for our people and our way of life more than you. But small pots of water boiling all day long to generate one cup to drink is not enough. I'm a farmer. You know this. But I can't make the soil produce crops without more water than the rains deliver."

He and I explained what we'd found.

"Wonderful." Madine clapped her hands. "This changes everything."

"Do your stories mention anything about how to bring the water to the top of the island?" I asked.

She frowned. "I don't believe they do."

"Let's take a look at this," Trilden said. "I'm willing to do that at least. Do I want to leave? No. Do I feel that I must? Yes."

With some trepidation, we took them down to the cave, others joining in until we had a large crowd following us. We showed them the big pool refilled already and boiling, plus the hood and how the condensed water trickled into the second tub.

"Taste it," Odik told those gathered around. "All of you."

"It's clean," someone exclaimed.

"It tastes wonderful!"

Madine smiled and nodded. With her cane, she pointed to the piping leaving the second tub, feeding into the wall. "I assume this uses some kind of gravity system to bring the water to the surface."

"The old pump near the center of town that has never worked," Trilden said. "Do you think . . ." He shook his head. "It's not possible, is it?"

"We should go find out," I said with a grin.

We returned to the surface, Madine riding on Odik's back because the climb was too steep. With lighter steps, we strode to the edge of town where it was clear there must've been large gardens long ago. Now only a few straggly vegetables have grown.

"It's over here." Trilden led everyone to the edge of the field and into the woods surrounding it. "I found it one day while looking for herbs, but as I said, it didn't work, so I ignored it after that." Bending down, he cleared away brush, revealing a pump like the one that brought sea water inside our homes. Straightening, he began lifting and dropping the lever. A hollow, gurgling sound rang out and Madine cheered.

"Will it work?" I asked Odik, leaning into his side.

He just shook his head, probably not wanting to say anything to jinx it.

Water gushed out of the pipe, splashing on the ground at Trilden's feet.

"What does it taste like?" someone asked.

Trilden cupped some in his hands and took a long drink. "I'd say . . ." He shot me and Odik a grin. "I'd say it tastes like a good reason to stay on the island."

Everyone around us cheered.

CHAPTER 30

ODIK

L ife suddenly felt easier on the island. Funny how a little thing like clean water could make all the difference.

Trilden and three other orcs left, but they'd be back. They'd gone to tell everyone about our discovery and urge any clansmales to move back home.

I was hoping once the island's population grew, we could expand services. A restaurant would be amazing, as would a market. And I had a feeling we'd draw healers and engineers to our laid-back way of life. The latter could study the desalination device and recreate others on different parts of the island.

"How did it go?" Eleri asked when I returned after a long day exploring to find other water pumps, then clear away brush and trees from around them. She sat at our table with sewing things spread out in every direction, working on a piece of clothing. She planned to create a complete wardrobe for each of us, then start making things ahead. She'd set up a shop here but also in the city. We could open it a few days per week and sell the clothing she'd made.

I'd tried to tell her we didn't need money, that all we needed was each other, but she'd insisted. Besides, she'd said, she loved sewing, and it would give her something to do in the evenings.

Frankly, I intended to monopolize as many of her evenings as I could, but I'd never take something from her that brought her joy.

"We found more pumps that draw water from the second pool," I said. "One is near our own garden."

"Wonderful." She set aside her sewing and came over to give me a kiss.

"A few of the males have gone to the city."

She froze in my arms. "Oh, no."

"It's good news. They took money with them to buy cattle. We'll arrange for a barge to bring them to the island where they can graze."

"Milk and meat?"

"Eventually."

"What else? I feel like so much has happened in a very short time."

"We're talking about building more homes for those who wish to move from the city. We'll expand the clan."

"How large a population do you think the island can support?" she asked.

"A few hundred. Others can live on the smaller islands, and we'll help them construct desalination devices to give them fresh water."

After we finished building new homes for future settlers, I had a plan for our own house. Two rooms at least, one for Eleri to use as a sewing room, and the other . . . Well, I wasn't going to say a thing about it. It would be a surprise for my mate.

To think this woman hadn't been in my life a short time ago. Now I couldn't imagine not seeing her each day, kissing her, and loving her all through the night.

"Would you like to go swimming?" I asked.

"I was going to make dinner."

"Let's catch our meal and roast it over a fire on the beach."

"Sounds wonderful. I picked more vegetables, and we can include them in our meal as well."

We left our home and started down the staircase, me carrying our fishing poles and bait, her a few vegetables.

"No more swimming naked," she said with a sigh. "With the cave so near, someone might see."

"You're right. The pool is too close to the cave."

When we reached the bottom of the stairs, I urged her to go left instead of right.

"Fishing first?" she asked.

"I thought we could do that after our swim."

"I'm going to have to wear a short dress from now on when I practice," she said with a pout, holding it aloft. She'd made it yesterday and modeled it for me, though honestly, she hadn't worn it for long.

I just grinned and led her around a bend, then another.

"Lots of walking tonight," she said with a smile.

"It'll be worth it."

One more turn, and we approached the smaller swimming hole I'd used a few times in the past.

"Aw, Odik," she exclaimed when we'd climbed the rocks and stood beside it. "No need for my short dress."

"Only if you wish."

"I know what *I'd* like." She sashayed up to me and teased her finger across my chest. My heart leaped up into my throat. "But what do *you* wish for, my love?"

"You, my mate. Always you."

CHAPTER 31

ODIK

I held my hands over Eleri's eyes.

"Can I see? Can I see?"

"Not yet," I said, my grin making my face ache.

"I haven't peeked. I promise." Joy came through in her voice, and it made me feel amazing to know I'd put it there. "You've been working on the house for a while, and I want to know what you're building."

I'd kept it secret.

Our discovery on the beach worked so well, everyone was putting in pumps to bring fresh water to the island's surface. I'd done the same of course, but I'd taken it even further. My mate had once expressed a wish, and I could do nothing else but fulfill her every desire.

We left the front of our house, and I guided her around to the side. I'd finish the doorway from the inside over the next few days, but my surprise would have more impact if we entered from this side.

"I'm going to fall," she said with a laugh, stretching her legs out one at a time to feel the ground before stepping forward.

"I won't allow that to happen."

"You think you'll be able to prevent it from happening?" She tripped, and I wrapped an arm around her waist, holding her snug against my chest.

At the same time, I shifted my other arm around to cover both of her eyes. "No peeking."

"You've been banging and making all kinds of noise for weeks," she huffed. "I swear, it's making it hard for me to focus on my sewing."

I proudly wore the pants and shirt she'd made me the first week, and she wore a lovely gown made of silky green fabric that hugged her generous curves. It was all I could do not to strip it off her the first time she modeled it for me. Maybe my upcoming surprise would help in that area.

I eased her to the right, taking the path I'd cleared to the detached building. At the door, I creaked it open and lifted her, placing her feet squarely on the newly laid wooden floorboards. Eventually, I'd build a breezeway between the two buildings, but for now, it stood alone, a testament to my dedication to my mate.

Inside, I brought her to a halt.

"Can I see?" she asked, laughter bubbling in her voice.

"You can." I lowered my arm and moved up beside her, watching her as she took in my surprise.

"A tub. A real tub?"

I chuckled. "It's not fake."

"You built me a bathhouse. Odik." She burst into tears.

I gulped and wasn't sure what to do. She enjoyed hugs, so I tugged her into my arms and held her while she sobbed. "I thought you'd be happy about this. Instead, I've made you sad."

"I am happy," she cried. "Really."

"Then why are you crying?"

"Because you did this for me, and I love you, and I think I'm pregnant."

I sucked in her words, and my heart came to a grinding halt. "You think you're pregnant?"

Nodding, she sniffed.

"Mate," I groaned. I swept her up and spun her around, kissing her as if my very life depended on it— which it did. "Mate. We're going to have an orcling together?"

"I hope so."

"A boy or a girl?"

She frowned. "There's no way to know that before it comes out."

"Maybe one of each."

"Twins?"

At her frown, I backtracked. "I'll settle for one at a time."

"Odik. I'm having one baby. One. Not two. At least not yet." She gave me a watery smile. "Show me the tub?"

"When you were newly arrived on the island, you

mentioned how wonderful it would be to have water piped into a tub. I decided cold water wouldn't do, so I rigged a system that heats the water as it emerges from the ground. I'll have to feed the heater with wood, but this way, you can take nice, warm baths whenever you want."

"So much work and for me?" She slid down my front until her feet touched the floor.

"I'll do anything for you, Eleri. You know that, don't you?"

She glanced at the tub. "There's one more thing you can do."

"What's that?"

"The tub looks large enough for two." She lifted her dress up over her head and carefully laid it on a nearby chair.

By the fates, she wore nothing underneath. Was she trying to kill me with lust? Whenever she wore the dress next, I'd be wondering if that was the day she'd chosen to wear underthings or the day she'd gone without.

I'd never get the image of her looking so lush and alluring out of my mind.

"I crafted the tub large on purpose," I gulped out.

She climbed the short steps and swung her legs over the side, sinking down into the steaming water I'd filled it with before I brought her out here. "Yes, there's plenty of room."

The smile she gave me made my heart ache with joy. This woman had brought light and color into my life, and there was no place I'd rather be than with her.

Curling her finger my way, she gave me a sultry smile. "Why don't you join me for our very first bath in our new tub?"

Eight Months Later

"One more," the orc midwife, Cassatine, called out. She'd moved to the island a few months ago to help one of the orc women with their first birth and decided to stay. With our population now over one hundred, and ten of them orcling-bearing aged females, we needed her more than those living in the city every would. They had more than enough healers to help with a birth.

"Push," she said again. "It's almost over, dear one, and your lovely orcling will join you and your mate."

"A boy or a girl?" I grated out as pain shot across my belly, bands tightening to help me deliver Odik's and my child.

"We'll know what it is soon," she said, wiping a cool cloth across my brow.

"Get Odik in here."

"This is a woman's place, not a male's. I'm afraid I cannot permit—"

"Now!"

Madine rose from the chair in the corner of the room. "Now, Eleri. Surely you don't want your big old orc husband in here when you deliver your precious orcling. He'll just be in the way."

"Odik," I barked. "Now."

"Very well." Madine chuckled as she left the room. "I do love her spunk."

Cassatine wrung out the cloth and wiped my face again while I groaned through another contraction.

Orclings grew large quickly, but with all the other human-orc matchups, they came out small. A saving grace for the women who birthed them.

"Eleri," Odik cried from the open doorway. He rushed into the room and climbed onto the bed beside me. "What do you need?"

"You." I held out my hand. "I'm about to deliver our child, and all I need is you holding my hand to make it happen."

"She just needs to push, actually," Cassatine said, though kindly.

"Push, love," Odik said. "Can you do that for me? It'll be over soon and our dear little orcling will join our family."

My belly rippled with another contraction.

"Argh," I cried, pushing while gripping Odik's hand as hard as I could.

He eased behind my back and held me, his fingers still linked with mine. "You're amazing, mate," he murmured in my ear. "One more. You can do it."

A gush and the head of our child exited my body, followed by the shoulders and the rest of our child's body. Birth could be a treacherous process, but it could also be the most wonderful experience in a woman's life.

"A boy," Cassatine crowed, lifting our child and laying him on my belly. Like all the other orclings birthed by women, he took after his father with rich, greenish-gold skin and tiny horns just nubs on his head.

"A boy," Odik said. "He's beautiful, mate. Just beautiful."

"He is, isn't he?" I stroked his soft hair, a rich black like his father's. "What would you like to name him?"

"How about Zur?"

Tears trickled down my cheeks at the thought. "Really?"

"Really. I owe everything to the man who raised you. He watched out for you, he cared for you. And I know you miss him."

"I do." I looked up at Odik. "I love you, mate."

He kissed me. "And I love you."

Cassatine wrapped Zur up in a clean cloth and handed him to me. Our son slept—for now.

She and Madine crept from the room, their faces creased with smiles.

And Odik and I snuggled with our new son.

I hope you enjoyed Eleri & Odik's story.
Would you like to read a bonus scene?
Their son, Zur, is now three, and he's in trouble!
Sign up for my newsletter,
& read now!

Visit with them five years from now in Orc's Craving,
the next book in the Monster Mate Hunt Series.

I've included the first chapter here . . .

ORC'S CRAVING

On the night of the Monster Mate Hunt, I'll be claimed as an orc's bride.

Rhoslyn

When my sister is chosen for the Monster Mate Hunt—an annual event where two women must sacrifice themselves to the orcs for the good of us all—I volunteer in her place. The orcs hunt me as I bolt through the forest. I'm captured by the gruff, growly Commander Jaus, who expects me to cook and clean, plus sleep in his quarters with him at night, despite insisting he doesn't want a mate.

Then something changes, and his dark, brooding gaze turns my way . . .

Jaus

Rhoslyn's beautiful, spitting mad, and determined never to be my bride. I take her to my home in the orc city, and in no time, I long for what I don't deserve—a mate and a life full of joy. When the city's attacked, and her life is in danger, I'll destroy everything just to protect her. I'm going to defeat our enemy, and then I'm going to make Rhoslyn mine.

Orc's Craving is Book 1 in the Monster Mate Hunt Series. Expect fated mates, found families, a distinctive size difference, and a "touch her and die" hero. Each book is standalone, but the series is best if read in order.

Books in Order:
Orc's Mate
(a prequel)
Orc's Craving
Orc's Fate
Orc's Maiden
Orc's Captive
Orc's Taming

Chapter One is next!

About the Author

Ava Ross is a two-time *USA Today* Bestselling author who has written numerous titles, all of them featuring sweet and steamy romance. She fell for men with unusual features when she first watched Star Wars, where alien creatures have gone mainstream. She lives in New England with her husband (who is sadly not an alien, though he is still cute in his own way), her kids, and a few assorted pets.

SERIES BY AVA

Mail-Order Brides of Crakair
Brides of Driegon
Fated Mates of the Ferlaern Warriors
Fated Mates of the Xilan Warriors
Holiday with a Cu'zod Warrior
Galaxy Games
Alien Warrior Abandoned/
Shattered Galaxies
Beastly Alien Boss
Bride of the Fae
A Sci-Fi Holiday Tail
Monsterville, USA
Monster on Board
(co-written with Alana Khan)
A Monster Worth Fighting For
(Monster Between the Sheets)
Love at First Orc
Monster Mate Hunt

Brides of the Zuldrux Warriors

Single Titles
A Monster Worth Fighting For
Craving Stardust
Dad Bod Dragon
Mated to the Dragon
Jasmine's Enchanted Genie
Swamp Thing (You Make My Heart Sing)

You can find my books on Amazon.

CHAPTER 1
RHOSLYN

A blood-ringed sun set on the evening of the Monster Hunt. Once darkness cloaked our world, two women from our village would leave the safety of the high fortress walls to become brides to vicious, powerful orcs.

No one knew for sure what happened after they stepped beyond the walls, because the women were never heard from again.

With my basket of herbs hooked over my arm, I hurried along the winding forest path that twisted like a serpent through the undergrowth. Sunlight pierced through the dense canopy above, casting eerie shadows that darted among the ancient trees. Silence loomed over the woods, broken only by my light footsteps, a random chirp of a bird, and the squawk of a squitt hiding among the upper branches overhead. Nature itself seemed to hold its breath.

It never paid to remain beyond the safety of the

fortress walls when darkness swallowed the world, and not just because of the Hunt.

The shaydes stalked us, hunting for food. We were their prey.

My knife gripped tightly in my hand, I left the depths of the forest and rushed across the broad grassy area between the woods and the high fortress walls.

Mine was the only village in this area, though I'd heard there were other villages far away. Only a few from my village had traveled in that direction, however.

Over a thousand humans hid beyond the ring of stone, relying on the fierce, enormous orcs who granted us protection from creatures even more dangerous than them in exchange for brides.

I slipped through the well-guarded door.

"Rhoslyn," the guardsman said with a glare, stomping forward. "Why do you challenge them like this?"

"What do you mean?" I asked breezily, slipping my knife into the sheath strapped about my waist and brushing evergreen needles from my long blue skirt. I'd collected those while digging roots at the base of the tree. "I found some willadon." I lifted the chunk of gnarly black root from my basket. "Now I can make more tea for your mother."

His lined face softened. "You're too kind to us all."

"I love brewing potions and making tinctures that help my friends."

"And what about Rhoslyn? What do *you* want for

yourself?" His pale blue eyes like my own softened, and his voice took on a fatherly tone.

I placed the root back in my basket with the herbs I was eager to dry. "I want to watch my sister marry the man she loves and spend the rest of my years bouncing her babies on my lap. And discover new uses for herbs."

"No marriage and bouncing babies for you?"

I winced. "I'm twenty-five. Who would have me?"

"Many. If you went to the village dances, you'd find a man to love."

"I don't need a man to make me feel complete."

"What about children? Surely you wish to raise young."

I did long for a child, but I'd yet to find anyone I dared give my heart to.

"Lyneth weds in a few months, does she not?" he asked.

Thinking of how happy my pretty sister would be with the man she loved, I grinned. "That's correct."

He patted my arm. "And then she'll move in with him and leave you alone. That would be the time to find your own husband."

My chin lifted. "I like being alone." Most of the time. Too often, I was lonely. "I plan to trade a tincture for a chall kit. The fluffy beast will make a nice companion."

"Indeed, the small creature will, but I haven't given up on you yet. Someone will offer for your hand." His warm gaze held appreciation, though it didn't feel slimy like—

Kael's eyes sharpened as he gazed past my shoulder.

Heavy footsteps approached, and my shoulders curled. If only I could sink beneath the cobblestones. I didn't need to turn; I knew who stalked closer.

I pivoted, my hand going to my knife, though I didn't pull it. That might get me into more trouble than I was eager to take on at the moment. But the last thing I wanted to do was present my back to Eamon, our village mayor.

"There you are, Rhoslyn." His greasy tone made my skin twitch.

Last night, this man cornered me in an alley and pressed his thick lips against mine. His hands roamed my body until I thrust my knee between his legs. With his barks of anger echoing around me, I rushed home, where I locked the door and leaned against it, trembling with rage and dismay.

Not long ago, he told me I'd soon be his bride.

He said he wouldn't ask permission, that he'd take me to his home, and no one would stand up for me.

He also told me if I didn't allow him to do as he pleased, he'd hurt my sister.

"I'm sorry, Eamon. I must return to my home right away." I held up the root, hoping he wouldn't see the quake in my hand. "Kael's mother needs her tea, or her body will ache all night." I forced a cheerful smile onto my face. "We wouldn't want to leave an elder in pain, now would we?"

Eamon huffed, and his gaze traveled down my curvy frame. "The women have been chosen."

Kael bristled, stomping his feet and clutching his

weapon. "We should tell the orcs no. We've sacrificed our women to them for ten years. It needs to end!"

"If we don't fulfill our side of the truce, the orcs will withdraw their protection." Dread coiled tightly around my heart. "We'll be overrun and consumed by the shayde before we can suck in a deep breath."

But did the fates help the woman claimed during the hunt?

Kael's shoulders slumped. He knew we had no choice. "Who must go into the woods tonight?" The fear in his voice told me he prayed one of the chosen wasn't his only daughter.

No one wished to become the mate of an orc. Why would they?

Our elders spoke of them in hushed whispers, and parents used tales of them to make their young behave. Some said they lived in splendor in a shining kingdom near the sea, while others said they were enormous, hideous beasts who lived in stark, damp caves.

They said that those claimed during the hunt were rutted until they became pregnant with an orcling. Once they gave birth, they'd be rutted again. Over and over until the day they died.

"Calita is the first. Her mother clings to her, but her father will see the deed done." Eamon's sly gaze met mine. "The name of the other woman who must leave the safety of the fortress and become the bride to an orc is being notified at this moment."

"Who is it?" Kael bellowed, his weapons clattering against his side.

The slick smile Eamon sent me made my pulse come to a jarring halt. My mouth went dry, and my throat clogged off with terror.

"No," I growled, knowing immediately who he meant. "Lyneth plans to wed soon."

"Lyneth will do as she's told." He chuckled, low and nasty. "The orcs won't care if she loves another when they capture her and claim her on the forest floor. I hear their bodies are large *everywhere*. That they don't take time to . . . shall we say, ensure a woman is eager to receive their favors."

Rage poured through me, making my face sting. Dropping my basket, I stomped over to him, sliding my knife from its sheath. If I gutted him this instant, I'd not only avoid lying beneath him on his bed one day soon, but I might also have a chance to save my sister. "I. Said. No!"

He backed up, his lips twisting. "It's not your decision, woman."

"It is if I volunteer for the hunt in her place."

Kael gasped. "No, Rhoslyn. You cannot."

"Anyone but Lyneth." I gripped my blade so hard it made my hand ache.

"You have no choice in this matter," Eamon said.

Oh, but there was always a choice. No one had ever volunteered, but there was nothing in the agreement that said a woman couldn't. I'd read the passage in the scrolls myself.

I sucked in a bitter breath and shoved it from my pinched lungs. "*I volunteer.*"

"Are you sure?" Eamon asked. "You may have a better offer to consider."

"I'd rather gut myself than marry *you*," I bit out.

"Very well, then." Eamon latched onto my arm and shoved me toward the gate, Kael followed, uselessly protesting. "The sun has nearly set. You must leave now."

My eyes stung with tears, and I struggled to break free of his grip. "But Lyneth. At least let me tell her goodbye."

"I'll tell her you took her place." Kael's warm gaze met mine. "I'll protect her too." He glared at Eamon. "She'll move in with me until she marries."

"Thank you." Breaking free of Eamon's biting nails, I hugged Kael, whispering a heartfelt plea. "Tell her I love her, would you? That I'll come back."

"I will." His face cratered with grief. He didn't need to name it. We all knew.

No women had ever returned from the hunt.

Get Orc's Craving Now!